Ginger Pye

Also by Eleanor Estes

PINKY PYE

THE WITCH FAMILY

THE MOFFATS
THE MIDDLE MOFFAT
RUFUS M.
THE MOFFAT MUSEUM

THE HUNDRED DRESSES
MIRANDA THE GREAT

Ginger
Pye

Eleanor Estes

WITH ILLUSTRATIONS BY
THE AUTHOR

AN ODYSSEY/HARCOURT YOUNG CLASSIC
HARCOURT, INC.
Orlando   Austin   New York   San Diego   London

Requests for permission to make copies of any part of the work should be
submitted online at www.harcourt.com/contact or mailed to the following address:
Permissions Department, Houghton Mifflin Harcourt Publishing Company,
6277 Sea Harbor Drive, Orlando, Florida 32887-6777.

First Harcourt Young Classics edition 2000
First Odyssey Classics edition 1990
First published 1951

www.HarcourtBooks.com

Library of Congress Cataloging-in-Publication Data
Estes, Eleanor, 1906–   .
Ginger Pye/Eleanor Estes; illustrated by the author.
p.   cm.
"An Odyssey/Harcourt Young Classic."
Summary: The disappearance of a new puppy named Ginger and
the appearance of a mysterious man in a mustard yellow hat
bring excitement into the lives of the Pye children.
[1. Dogs—Fiction.   2. Brothers and sisters—Fiction.]   I. Title.
PZ7.E749Gi   2000
[Fic]—dc21   00-26700
ISBN 978-0-15-202499-4   ISBN 978-0-15-202505-2 (pb)

Printed in the United States of America
I   K   M   O   P   N   L   J
V   X   Z   BB   CC   AA   Y   W   (p b)

To Cici and Gretchen

CONTENTS

1

The Pyes and Pets

Would Gracie-the-cat be jealous if the Pyes got another pet—a dog? That was what Jerry Pye wanted to know and what he was dreaming about as he sat with Rachel, his sister, on their little upstairs veranda. Gracie had belonged to the family for eleven years. This was longer than Rachel, aged nine, or even Jerry, aged ten, had. She had been a wedding present to Mama, and she was known in the neighborhood as "the New York Cat." Jerry was trying to imagine what Gracie's feelings would be if the Pyes did get another pet—a dog.

The one thing that Jerry Pye wanted more than anything else in the world right now was a dog. Ever since he had seen the new puppies over in Speedys' barn, he was not only more anxious than ever to have a dog, he was most anxious to have one of these Speedy puppies. He had the particular one picked out that he would most like to have as his own. This was not easy to do for they were all wonderful.

Jerry had chosen this certain special puppy because he was convinced he was the smartest of the new puppies. Naturally, he would love any dog he had, but imagine owning such a smart puppy as this one! When he owned him he would teach him to heel, be dead dog, sneeze, scratch his stomach when Jerry scratched his back, beg, and walk on his hind legs. *If* he had this dog, that is. And he looked speculatively at Gracie-the-cat who had pushed open the screen door and was now lolling with an agreeable expression on the rope mat. He would not want to hurt her feelings and he thought some more whether it would or would not hurt Gracie's feelings if he brought a puppy into the house.

It was a Friday evening and Jerry and Rachel had been sitting, reading, on the little upstairs veranda of their tall house. Rachel had *The Secret Garden* from the library, and Jerry had one of the Altsheler books, and neither one of these books was an "I" book. They both always opened a book eagerly and suspiciously looking first to see whether or not it was an "I" book. If it were they would put it aside, not reading it until there was absolutely nothing else. Then, at last, they would read it. But, being an "I" book, it had to be awfully good for them to like it. Only a few, *Robinson Crusoe, Treasure Island*, and *Swiss Family Robinson*, for example, survived the hard "I" book test. These were among their best beloved in spite of the obvious handicap.

The children had read for a long time, but then it had grown dark. Now they were just sitting quietly, thinking, and watching the bats and bugs hurl themselves against the tall streetlamp which had suddenly come on and was casting a purple glow. Jerry was getting ready to bring up the matter of the dog to discuss with his sister Rachel, but first he liked to sit and dream about the wonderful idea that it was.

Rachel and Jared, called Jerry, Pye were very close companions. Of course they had many friends too; for instance, Dick Badger, who lived next door and who had a huge gray hound that knew how to scratch its stomach when you scratched its back, was Jerry's best friend.

Rachel's best friend was a girl over on Bugle Street named Addie Egan. All the boys and girls in Grade Five said Addie Egan had cooties and she really did not have cooties at all. Rachel stuck up for Addie whenever the occasion arose and she said,

"Let Addie sign your character books. She does not have cooties."

But then Rachel stuck up for everybody who was picked on. There was a little girl named Evvie Powers in the next block and sometimes the older boys and girls picked on her. "Police! Come and get Evvie!" they would cry, trying to scare the wits out of Evvie. But Rachel, if she heard them, would cry out, "Police! Don't come and get Evvie!" And she would run and put her arms around the little girl. Evvie just worshiped Rachel and wanted to be with her every minute. This was a nuisance, for Evvie wasn't even up to onesies in the game of onesie-twosie and Rachel was up to fivesies! But Evvie had to be protected nevertheless. Rachel would give her a smile and a pat and say, "Don't worry, Evvie. I won't let the police get you." Then she would run off to find Addie or Jerry and Dick or someone her age, leaving Evvie wiping her eyes and looking after her adoringly.

Rachel was an eager skinny little girl who almost always wore skirts and blouses that didn't stay tucked in, or sweaters, and her nose was frequently runny, because she had hay fever. Jerry was skinny too, but his nose didn't run. Jerry had black hair and Rachel's was reddish gold though, at this moment, sitting under the streetlamp, the hair of both of them looked purple.

To lead up to the subject that was nearest his heart Jerry said, "Rache, which is more important— a dog or a cat?"

Rachel and Jerry were in the habit of having discussions as to what was the most important of anything—the most important, or the prettiest, or the best, or the funniest. For instance, in the dictionary, almost their only picture book except for Mr. Pye's books of birds, they had excited discussions over which was the prettiest fish on the shiny colored page of fish, or the prettiest bird, or butterfly. One favorite discussion of theirs was the one they had whenever they played train, calling out like conductors, "New York to Boston!" Which was more important, they asked one another, New York or Boston?

"New York," Jerry would say. "Because it has the Museum of Natural History in it."

"Boston," said Rachel. "Because it sounds more important."

"Why?"

"It just does."

Rachel couldn't explain the reason she thought Boston sounded more important than New York but it probably had something to do with the roundness of the letters, the *B* and the *o*'s. For the same reason she thought London sounded more important than Paris, though Paris sounded prettier. Sometimes, since Jerry was one year older than she, she wondered if she, too, should not say, "New York." Still, to her, Boston sounded rounder, bigger, more solid—more important.

Their town, Cranbury, was between these two big cities. The trains went streaking past, running back and forth from Boston to New York, from New York to Boston. Mama was from a little town near New York, and Papa was from Boston. This made it doubly hard to choose the more important. How had Mama met Papa when they were at two different ends of the railroad?

It happened this way. Papa was much older than Mama. He was thirty-five when he met Mama and up till then he had not had a minute to get married because all he thought about was birds, birds, birds. Already, he was a quite famous bird man. Well, one day Papa happened to be standing in a New York subway station. Though he came from Boston he had frequent business in New York. In this particular subway station there was an escalator and all of a sudden Papa decided to see if he could run up the escalator, not the "up" escalator, the "down" one. He would have to run pretty fast to beat the stairs that were trying to bring him back downwards. Papa said he had always wanted to try this but naturally he did not want to make a fool of himself in front of other people of whom there were plenty in New York. This time, however, there weren't any other people around and it was a splendid opportunity. So. Up he flew, several steps at a time, and he did manage to reach the top.

It so happened that when, panting, Papa did reach the top, there was a certain young girl who was about to come down the escalator; and here Papa came racing up it so fast, he couldn't help it. He knocked the young lady down. Now this girl happened to be Mama who had come to the city for the opera matinee. The opera was *Tannhäuser*, the first she had ever seen, and she was floating through the air, almost, she was so transported by the magnificent music, when all of a sudden she landed flat on her back, knocked over by this crazy man who was flying up the "down" escalator.

Well, of course, since Mama was such a young little thing and wore only a size two shoe, and, moreover, ate like a bird, Papa had to marry her. They fell in love at first sight and though she was

only seventeen, they got married as soon as all the permissions could be granted.

It was the most interesting way for a mother to meet a father of any that Rachel and Jerry had heard so far. Addie Egan's mother had met her father at the high school prom, for example. And Dick Badger's mother had met his father at a Sunday school picnic. And so it went. At any rate this was how it happened that Rachel and Jerry had the youngest mother in the town of Cranbury, and the youngest grandmother, and the youngest uncle, their Uncle Bennie, Mama's baby brother, who was now only three years old.

Papa and Mama came to Cranbury to live so that Papa could study the birds of the marshes and the woods and the fields, and because Cranbury was in the middle between New York and Boston. Perhaps they, too, could not make up their minds which was more important, New York or Boston, and had to settle halfway.

After a while Gramma and Grampa moved to Cranbury too, so that Uncle Bennie would grow up knowing his niece and nephew, Rachel and Jerry, and none of them be strangers to any of them. Grampa was a piano tuner and he said he'd just as lief tune pianos in Cranbury as where he was and moreover he could have a boat in Cranbury, which he couldn't in New York. Sometimes Rachel and Jerry asked Grampa which he thought was more important, New York or Boston, and between plinking the piano keys, he'd say, "New York." But then, naturally, being from there he could not be a traitor and say, "Boston."

After Rachel had been taken to visit both cities,

New York and Boston, finding them both wonderful, she didn't know what to say in the importance game. To keep it interesting, however, she continued to say, "Boston." What would be the sense of both her and Jerry saying, "New York"? There would not have been any game then. And, anyway, the name, "Boston," still *sounded* more important.

It was Papa who had taken Rachel on her first visit to Boston. And it was Mama who had taken her on her first visit to New York. The time she went to Boston with Papa happened to be over the Thanksgiving weekend, just a few years before this story begins. They were to spend the weekend with an old aunt of Papa's, Auntie Hoyt, who had been the first to steer Papa toward birds. She was a spinster aunt and she was very old and fragile and Papa was very fond of her.

That weekend was a cold, raw, and bleak one. Rachel slept on a small cot in the parlor and she could not get warm the whole night. She didn't have enough covers and her feet would not warm up. She stayed awake and stayed awake and though she scrunched herself up into a tight ball, she still stayed cold. Since Auntie Hoyt was poor, Rachel imagined she did not have any more covers in the cupboard and she felt she should not embarrass her by asking for more. Anyway she didn't want to be a nuisance and wake anybody up, so she shivered and shook. Also she didn't want Papa to think he had such a cold daughter he could not possibly take her on any more trips. Rachel longed to go on bird trips with Papa, to the coldest North and the hottest South and

traipse through the swamps of Florida. She had to be stoic. It must have been about three in the morning before she ever fell asleep.

The next night as Rachel got ready for bed she viewed the cold couch of night with horror. She felt she could not stand the cold another minute. Papa was reading *The Auk*, and Auntie Hoyt a little book of *Forget-me-nots*. Whispering, so Auntie Hoyt would not hear her, and hoping the question would not fill Papa with such disgust he would never take her to Labrador, she asked Papa where they had hung her overcoat—she planned to sleep in it. Then he and Auntie Hoyt, who *had* heard, were sorry and piled a hundred coats on her couch. She was still cold, however, and could not get her feet warm the whole time she was there, in Boston.

In Boston, one day, she had an unusual experience. While Papa and Auntie Hoyt waited out of sight somewhere, she had to go by herself into a large room in a department store and listen to someone dressed up like Santa Claus read a Christmas story and *'Twas the night before Christmas*. This seemed odd to her for at Thanksgiving time, she was not ready for Santa Claus. In Cranbury they got through the turkeys and the pumpkins and the Pilgrims before they brought out the Santa Clauses.

She was quite relieved when the whole occasion was over and instead of being abandoned she found Papa and Auntie Hoyt waiting, beaming, at the door.

They went on an underground trolley car in Boston which went too fast around corners and it was a wonder it did not bump into the wall. For almost every meal Auntie Hoyt gave them baked beans out of a can and cold boiled ham both of which Rachel was very fond of but for which Auntie Hoyt apologized, saying hard times had hit her. In Boston, she also saw the Common, the old North church, the Bunker Hill monument, and where John Adams was buried. It was all like walking through the pages of the history book. Could New York come up to this?

The following year when Mama took her down to New York, she saw that it could, but in a different way. It is true she had a number of ideas about New York before she got there which came in for quite a reshuffling when she saw how things really were. For instance, she had expected the elevated railway to be a little train running on narrow tracks from pole to pole about a half a mile in the air, really elevated. A sky train, she had thought, reached perhaps by ladder, and she had anticipated riding on it with the greatest delight. On the contrary the elevated was so low down, the trolleys that ran over

the viaduct from Cranbury to the city were almost as exciting.

The subway, too, was not as she had expected. She had thought a subway would be a shining thing way way down in the middle of the earth. But there, one had merely to go down a flight of stairs and one beheld the subway; and she did not see the escalator that Papa flew up.

But in New York Rachel tasted the best meal she ever had in her whole life. She and Mama had walked for miles and miles and hours and hours. They had had nothing to eat because on the train

Rachel had eaten up the hard-boiled egg sandwiches that were supposed to be eaten in some quiet park with the squirrels and pigeons. Her footsteps lagged; she was hot, hungry, and tired. Finally her mother caught on and took her into a long, narrow store—she said afterwards it was the five-and-ten-cent store—and there Rachel was served this delicious dinner of pot roast and mashed potatoes and gravy and peas, and not too much, just enough, on a thick little hard white plate. Her dinner cost ten cents, Mama said, and it impressed Rachel that for either five or ten cents, one could buy almost anything in New York.

Even dresses. For after this wonderful little dinner they went into an enormous place and there, for ten cents apiece, Mama bought Rachel two dresses, a blue one and a brown one, and these were the first bought dresses Rachel had ever had. Mama made all her clothes. Rachel loved the bought dresses. But when they were washed they shrank up to nothing and she had to give them to Thelma Ruby, her old doll.

These were the only times so far that Rachel had been to either New York or Boston and when they played the game as to which was more important she still said, "Boston," so there'd be a game.

"Which is more important?" asked Jerry again for it seemed that Rachel had not heard the first time. "A cat or a dog?"

"Both," said Rachel, for this was like asking which was more important, a girl or a boy, and could not be answered.

"M-m-m," said Jerry.

September breezes stirred the branches of the huge horse chestnut tree that hung over the house; the stars were coming out; and the two children sat in silence. Then, stepping carefully over Gracie, not to make her move, Rachel reached for a horse chestnut that was glistening in the lamplight and, polishing it on her skirt, she sat down again on the bench beside Jerry. In the distance shouts of children playing hide-and-seek could be heard. Then, because it looked as though Rachel might possibly have it in mind to get up and run around the corner and get in the hide-and-seek game, to keep her here, Jerry said, "Hey."

"M-m-m?" said Rachel, sitting down again.

"I been thinking."

"M-m-m," said Rachel. And she waited. Thinking was more in Jerry's line than talking, but finally he blurted out:

"Would Gracie be jealous if we had another pet, a dog?"

"A dog!" exclaimed Rachel in surprise.

"Yes, a dog. There's a puppy over at Speedys' barn and they said I could have him for one dollar."

"One dollar!" said Rachel. "Where'd you get the dollar?"

"First," said Jerry. "Would Gracie be jealous, that's what I'm asking you. Not, where'd I get the dollar."

Well. There was silence for a few minutes while Rachel took this in. Then she said incredulously, "Is Gracie a pet?"

Neither Rachel nor Jerry ever petted Gracie because Gracie had no use for children, imagining they were just out to pull her tail. It is hard to know how she got this wrong idea, but she did have it, and the only person she had any use for was Mama. When she caught a rat out in the barn, as she did once in a while, she brought it to Mama, laying it proudly at Mama's feet. If Mama did not act as pleased as Gracie expected, she would neatly rip the rat's stomach open with her claws so Mama would find it more tempting. This performance, however unpleasant, was remarkable, and Mrs. Pye boasted of it to all other cat owners who were not too squeamish to hear the tale.

Naturally, the feelings of such an important cat and her position in the household had to be carefully considered before taking such a step as Jerry had suggested.

"Is Gracie a pet?" Rachel repeated.

"Of course she's a pet. If she's a cat, she's a pet."

"Oh. I thought she was a member of the family."

"She is. But she's still a pet."

So now they were back at the beginning. Would Gracie, being a pet of the Pyes, be jealous if Jerry brought this puppy of the Speedys into the house?

"Well," said Rachel, counting on her fingers to make her answer more important. "There are four of us and none of us is jealous because there is more than one of us."

"But we're people. I'm not talking about getting another people. I'm talking about a dog."

"I don't think Gracie would be jealous of a dog," reasoned Rachel carefully. "Because we're not jealous of Gracie. And we're people and she's a cat. And she'll think about the dog the way we think about her. She might be jealous if we got another cat, like we might be jealous if we got another people. But she won't be jealous if we get a dog, any more than we would be."

This sounded rather sensible to Jerry and he looked at his sister gratefully.

"Did you ask Mama?" asked Rachel.

"No," said Jerry. "First I had to find out if Gracie would be jealous."

Presently Mama came out for a breath or two of air. She sat down in the little old red wooden rocker and fanned herself with a folded newspaper. Then Jerry told her he had a plan to buy this certain puppy of the Speedys for one dollar since Gracie, as Rachel said, being a member of the family and a cat, would not be jealous of their having a new pet—a dog.

"A dog!" said Mama, and Rachel and Jerry saw with satisfaction that she showed the proper surprise. "Well," she said. There had never been a dog in the Pye family before, only Mama and Papa and Jerry and Rachel and Gracie. Naturally it came as a jolt to try to imagine life with a dog when life had been going along so long without one.

But Mama did not hesitate long. She said that it would be very nice to have a dog and, since Mama was Mama, she did not ask Jerry where he was going to get the dollar. Rachel did though. She asked again where Jerry was going to get the dollar. Jerry muttered he wasn't sure just yet so Rachel knew it was going to be a hard thing to do.

It seemed to Rachel that by the time Jerry could get a whole dollar saved up the puppy would be a grown-up dog. If he had only told them sooner they could have begun to save long ago. They could have made mite boxes such as those given out in Sunday school during Lent, and she and Jerry could have put their pennies in them. Soon there might have been enough to buy the dog. This way though, since he had not told them until now, and since they did not want this puppy to be a grown-up dog before they got him, they would have to think of some quicker plan.

Naturally Rachel would help Jerry get the dollar, only she just couldn't think how, aside from the mite boxes which were the only idea that had occurred to her so far. Even if there had been time for mite boxes they were not such a good idea after all, she corrected herself. She had guiltily remembered the way hers always looked when she turned it in in Sunday school, the slot for the pennies all stretched and torn from taking pennies out again. It was not a neat and tidy mite box the way Beulah Ball's was; it was a dirty, torn, loose mite box, and so was Jerry's.

To tell the truth Jerry was not at all certain how he was going to earn that dollar either but he did not doubt that he would find some way. If Papa's book that he was writing on birds sold a lot of copies

Jerry could ask Papa for the dollar. But it would be a long time before that was finished. The puppy would certainly be grown up and belonging to someone else long before then. The book probably would not sell a lot of copies anyway. It was for scholars.

Papa was a great bird man and for a few minutes Jerry thought proudly about him. He was off now on a trip to the Everglades to study birds in their habitat there. Men in Washington were always quoting Mr. Pye's articles on birds. When some question on the conservation of birds came up, "Call in Mr. Pye," was the first thing the men in Washington said. They would pay his fare to Washington but that was all they would pay aside from the respect.

Outside of the family and the ladies of the Far and Near Society, who subscribed to the *National Geographic* and frequently saw his name in print, few people in Cranbury knew that Mr. Pye was such a famous bird man; for of course he did not run around saying, "I, I, I."

It was thought that since Mr. Pye did not work in an office or a factory, and did not teach school either, he must naturally be wealthy, traveling all around the way he did. Nothing could have been further from the truth. His pocket and Mama's pocketbook were almost always practically empty. So

getting the dollar for the puppy from Mama or Papa was not to be considered.

Rachel was thinking about Papa too. The way he loves birds! she thought. He could not bear to think of harm coming to any of them and he pleaded with his neighbors to put bells around their cats' necks, the way Gracie had around hers. There were more belled cats in this neighborhood than anywhere else in Cranbury and, maybe, the world.

One day Papa read in the paper that birds had rained on New York City, little birds that had missed their course in migration and bumped into the high buildings. Hundreds died. Papa had not been able to eat or sleep. He took a train down to New York to study the whole sad matter and make a report on it. "The way Papa loves birds is the way I love, the way I love . . ." Rachel thought hard. "The way I love birds, too." She remembered she was going to be a bird man just like Papa when she grew up. She would accompany Papa on his bird trips and when the big fellows in Washington said, "Call in Mr. Pye," they would add, "And his little girl."

Whereas Rachel collected bird nests and feathers and anything to do with birds that she could find, Jerry collected stones and rocks, and his room was filled with them.

Picking up a rock, when she and Jerry were on a searching expedition, Rachel would ask, "Is this quartz?"

"No," Jerry would say.

"What is it then?" asked Rachel, because Jerry was going to be a rock man, a quartz man, when he grew up and he knew everything.

"It's just plain rock," answered Jerry.

"One thing," said Jerry so suddenly Rachel started. Her thinking had wandered far from the puppy and how Jerry was going to get the dollar.

"M-m-m," she said.

"This puppy that I'm going to buy for one dollar that was born in Speedys' barn had his tail cut off yesterday. They all did."

"His tail cut off!" said Rachel, horrified. "Didn't it hurt? And he's not a whole dog then? He should cost less than one dollar."

Mama said quickly, "They know how to cut off puppy dogs' tails so fast it doesn't hurt at all and it helps the beauty of them when they grow up not to have the long lanky tail."

"Most dogs I know have tails," said Rachel.

"Not fox terriers," said Jerry.

"I thought they were born without them."

"No. Anyway it didn't hurt, Mama said," affirmed Jerry rather doubtfully for this was hard to take in.

Since it had grown cooler, Mama went into the house to get some typing done on one of Papa's articles on birds, this one—*The terns*; and soon, clickety-clickety, they could hear her racing along. Rachel and Jerry sat awhile longer wondering how they could earn a dollar.

Jerry had only until tomorrow night at six o'clock to raise the dollar because Mrs. Speedy said so. She said, "I'd like for you to have this puppy you're so crazy about, Jerry. But there's someone else wants him too. And he keeps after me, you bet." Mrs. Speedy always put a great many "you bets" into her conversation and the Pyes all called her "Mrs. Speedy, you bet," or just plain, "You bet."

"He's always hanging around, this other fellow, waving the dollar," Mrs. Speedy told Jerry and the words were harping in his ears now. She also said, "I said to him, I said, if Jerry is not here by six o'clock Saturday then you can have the puppy. You bet."

When Jerry told Rachel this, she whistled. "Phew," she said. "We only have tonight and to-morrow."

But the evening came to an end, and they went

to bed with no idea how the dollar was to be earned. The only thing that was settled was that Gracie-the-cat would probably not be jealous, that and the fact that Mama said it would be all right for them to have a dog. But there was all day tomorrow and something would surely happen.

At night, when Jerry and Rachel went to bed they had the habit of making up stories, or rather one long continuous story that never ended. This story was all about the adventures of Martin Boombernickles, a character that could change itself into a horse, a boy, a man, a dog, anything, whenever it felt like it. They almost never went to sleep without adding an episode.

It was cozy in the night to hear Jerry call out from his narrow iron bed in his room, to Rachel in her narrow iron bed in her room, the next room, "Rachel, are you asleep? We haven't done the episode yet."

Rachel never went to sleep before Jerry even though she was a whole year younger, pinching herself to stay awake, if necessary, in order not to miss adding to the story. In delight, she would call out, "No. Oh, Boombernickles." Because it was the one who said "Boombernickles" first who was allowed to commence the episode.

Boombernickles had been going on for years and years. It was Rachel who had named it. "Oh, Boombernickles," she used always to say whenever she had to do something she didn't particularly like.

"Wherever did you get that word, boombernickles?" her mother asked.

"I don't know," said Rachel. But "Boombernickles" came to be the name of the character that could do anything, *anything*, in the nighttime stories she and Jerry made up.

Tonight, after the episode was finished, before he went to sleep, Jerry said, "Rache. I'll get the puppy, won't I? Something'll happen. I'll get the dollar, won't I?"

"Sure," muttered Rachel drowsily. "Something'll happen."

2

Dusting the Pews

Something did happen the next day, but not until Jerry had begun to feel very worried about his dog and his dollar. It was a hot day. Gramma had come early in the morning and left Uncle Bennie with the Pyes. From a long way off they could always hear Gramma pushing Uncle Bennie in his go-cart because it had a squeak in it, or pulling him in his express wagon which also had a squeak in it and in which he had arrived today.

Now, it was twelve o'clock noon. During the morning Jerry had exhausted all the possible ways he knew of to earn a dollar in one day. He had even offered to wash Mrs. Carruthers' windows—they were very dirty. But she said, "No." She did them herself twice a year and it was not time to do them for this half the year yet.

Jerry still had the afternoon, of course. But Saturday afternoon was never a good time for odd jobs. Saturday morning was, but not Saturday afternoon. On Saturday afternoon the men were likely to be home, the smell of tobacco would be wafted from the homes, and either the men would be napping on their couches, their shoes off and their old coats on, or else they would be digging and poking in the earth and leaves. It was useless to look for an odd job on Saturday afternoon.

Still, there were six hours to go before the puppy would be lost to them forevermore. Uncle Bennie and Jerry and Rachel were having their lunch. They had vegetable soup because Mama believed in something hot in the stomach even on warm days. And then they had applesauce. For Uncle Bennie's amusement Mama sang a little song. She sang:

> "Brother Morgan plays the organ,
>   Father plays the drum,
>   Sister plays the tamborina,
>   And Baby goes bum bum bum."

To show his appreciation Uncle Bennie counted for them, up to ten. "One, two, three, GO, five, six, seven, eight, nine, ten."

He always said, "Go," after "three," instead of

"four" because when he was swinging or getting ready to race with Jerry and Rachel, they always said, "One, two, three, GO!" Naturally he thought go came after three and that was where he always put it, in counting.

Uncle Bennie was famous in Cranbury. He was a hero because here he was, only three years old, and yet he was an uncle. All the children came and gaped at him when he came to visit Jerry and Rachel, which was just about every Saturday. His mother, who was Jerry and Rachel's grandmother, would leave him at the Pyes' when she went to town to do the marketing, and children in the neighborhood would gather around and study Uncle Bennie because he was an uncle at the age of three.

He was given special privileges and allowed to do things with the older children even though he was still practically a baby, all on account of being an uncle. "A venerable uncle," said Mrs. Badger, the next-door neighbor. "God keep him," she would say. Uncle Bennie could go anywhere he liked with the older boys and girls merely because he was an uncle.

"Play with the children your own age," his mother would plead, expecting he would get knocked down. "Play with the children your own age."

"Not innerested," said Uncle Bennie.

Or, "Take a little nap," she'd plead. "Take a little nap." (Most grown-ups said things twice to Uncle Bennie thinking, wrongly, that since he was so little, he would not have heard the first time.)

"Not innerested," he'd say. You'd think he was a grown-up man, the way he did not like to take naps.

Because he was a baby uncle, Bennie usually got the best of everything. At the Stokeses' big birthday party, to which almost all the children of Cranbury were invited, the ice cream served was molded into different interesting shapes. And Uncle Bennie got the most exciting ice cream of all. Mrs. Stokes thought of what was right for everybody and since Uncle Bennie lived over near the water and loved to watch the steamboat, the *Richard Peck*, he was given an ice cream steamboat!

At this party Rachel got a bird ice cream because of her father, not because of herself, because no one in town knew she was going to be a bird man when she grew up. But Mrs. Stokes belonged to the Far and Near Society and she knew how famous a bird man Mr. Pye was. So she had given Rachel an ice cream robin, chocolate on top and orange ice beneath. To Jerry, since likewise, no one in town knew he was going to be a rock man, she just happened to give a pickax. Imagine an ice cream pickax! But that he had. It was eerie the way Mrs. Stokes had everything figured. But Uncle Bennie's steamboat attracted the most oh's and ah's.

"What's your name?" people would say to Bennie.

"Uncle Bennie," he would answer. And like as not someone would give him a nickel or a penny merely for being an uncle. It was the easiest way of picking up pennies Jerry had ever heard of. But it certainly was not the solution to his picking up one hundred of them for the puppy he wanted to buy at Speedys' barn, and he puckered his brow and considered.

Lunch was over. Where could Jerry turn now to earn his dollar? He didn't know. And just as he was thinking, disconsolately, that he would run over to Speedys' barn and stay with his puppy until the very last minute, just then a miracle happened.

A tall boy named Sam Doody, who lived a few doors away in their block, came and knocked at the kitchen door. Sam Doody was about fifteen years old and he was so tall that every time any little boy or girl met him they always asked him how the air was up there. Sam had heard this joke so often he must have been very tired of it. But he was very good-natured and he always grinned and said, "Swell!"

Sam Doody and Judge Ball and a man named Mr. Tuttle were the three tallest people in the church. Sitting, they all towered above everybody else. Standing, Sam Doody and Judge Ball still towered. But Mr. Tuttle shrank and mingled with the congregation for his tallness was only from the waist up. From the waist down he was very short. Anyway Sam Doody was tall from top to toe and Uncle Bennie was nearly falling over backwards now trying to see top.

Well, Sam Doody, the tall boy, had a job on Saturdays dusting the pews of the church and now he said to Jerry, "Hey, Jerry. How'd you like to earn a dollar this afternoon?"

Jerry nearly fell flat. It sounded like a joke to him. Here he was wondering how he could earn a dollar and here was Sam, the tall boy, asking him how he'd like to earn a dollar. He was speechless waiting to see if it was a joke, or what.

"I have to go to town to buy a new suit, and I thought if you'd do me this favor, I'd give you the dollar I always get for dusting the pews. Because that's what I want you to do, dust the pews."

Jerry nodded his head up and down slowly. He was still too speechless for anything else and he wished the tall boy would sit down so he could see his face better and study whether this was a joke or not. He was also remembering Sam Doody's first suit with long pants. It was a dark green suit and when he walked into church with it on, everybody knew it was Sam Doody's new suit with long pants, his first suit with long pants, which was why his face was red.

Rachel, too, was remembering the first suit of Sam Doody's that had long pants to it, and she asked him if he was going to get another dark green suit. She liked that other suit, she said. And Sam Doody said he didn't know.

Jerry glared at Rachel. She shouldn't be asking a big fellow like Sam Doody what color suit he was going to buy. Sam Doody was captain of the high school basketball team. He was so tall he could practically put the ball into the basket just standing on his tiptoes. He was one of the most important people in Cranbury and here Rachel was, asking him what color suit he'd buy. It was a wonder Sam Doody didn't walk out of the kitchen and out of the door and say, "Forget the pews and the dollar, fellow." But he didn't. He was still smiling, showing his white, white teeth, and he said, "Well, how about it, fellow? Dust the pews for me?"

Again Jerry nodded. How could he say anything?

Sometime he would tell Sam Doody how this dollar happened to buy the smartest puppy in all of Cranbury for him. He longed to ask Sam when he would get the dollar. Would it possibly be before six o'clock tonight? But of course he could not ask such a question. Moreover, he thought he could run over to Mrs. Speedy's before the dusting of the pews and explain to her that he had the dollar, that all he had to do was dust some pews, that is, and then the dollar would be his. And he would ask her to please not sell the puppy to that other person, whoever he was, even though that other person might have the dollar right in his pocket.

"OK then," said Sam Doody and turned to go, nearly stepping on Uncle Bennie. "Hello there, Uncle Bennie," he said, grinning. "Where's your bubbah?"

"Bubbah" was Uncle Bennie's name for an old pink blanket he loved and used always to carry around with him. In fact, he considered Bubbah a member of the family and always said, "Mommy, Daddy, Uncle Bennie, and Bubbah," when people asked him who was in his family.

"Too big to take Bubbah with me now," he said, a little sadly.

"Well, you hang on to Bubbah anyway," said

Sam Doody and then, going out the door, he said, "Better get over to the church soon, Jerry. And don't forget the choir stalls and the pulpit," he cautioned. "Oh, and pay special attention to old Mrs. Widdemeyer's pew, will you? One thing she can't stand is a speck of dust on her pew."

Jerry said, "I'll dust it good," and Sam was gone.

Hardly had Sam gone, however, when his long legs brought him right back. "Here," he said. "Might as well pay you the dollar now, in case I should forget."

"Jiminy crickets!" exclaimed Jerry and, when Sam had really left for good, he fell down on the floor in a pretended faint, blew whistle notes on his fingers, and wrestled a bit with Uncle Bennie. "He's a first class Boy Scout, an Eagle Scout," said Jerry, almost sobbing in admiration, awestricken at the years of learning and accomplishment that had gone into the formation of this perfect person, Sam Doody. When he was Sam Doody's age and height, he would carry dollar bills around with him in his pocket and hire boys like Jerry to dust pews so they could buy dogs or rabbits.

"The Boy Scout boy, the Boy Scout boy," chanted Uncle Bennie, clapping his hands.

"Well," said Jerry importantly. "I better get to work." The pews were never to have such a dusting as this was going to be.

It had never before occurred to Rachel that a church had to be dusted. She had never thought that a church might get dirty. If she had, she would then never have imagined that ordinary people like herself and Sam Doody would do the dusting. She would have imagined the dusters would have to be superior beings, angels perhaps.

"Want me to help?" asked Rachel anxiously. She did so want to help dust the pews. She imagined this would be a great experience, not at all like dusting the black horsehair furniture in their parlor. It would be interesting, too, to be in church dusting pews on a Saturday when no one else was there. It would be like being behind the scenes at the Town Hall when she was in a play. She might see God.

"Sure," said Jerry, glad to have company.

Then it seemed that Uncle Bennie must go along also because he was to spend the whole day with Jerry and Rachel. Instead of Gramma coming for him later in the day she wanted Jerry and Rachel to bring him home around six o'clock. She lived a long way off, over by the water, and Rachel and Jerry could have supper there, she said. So. First they'd dust the pews, then they'd get the puppy, then they'd take Uncle Bennie home and have some supper, then they'd go home themselves, with the puppy. That's what they would do.

They put Uncle Bennie in his wagon and dragged him lickety-cut down the street, not stopping to look at anything—the fire engine house, *anything*. When they reached the pretty stone church on the Green,

Jerry was glad to see that the doors were open. He had been wondering how he was going to open the heavy brown doors and tall Sam Doody had not told him exactly what to do, except where he would find the dusters in the Parish House.

These he and Rachel found easily enough and once they had persuaded Uncle Bennie to leave his wagon outside, saying he could not ride it up and down the cement aisle—this was church and he must tiptoe and be quiet—they got to work, each one with a big cloth duster. Since Rachel had neglected to bring a hat, she had to put her handkerchief on her head. To hold this on with one hand and to dust with the other was difficult.

"This my bubbah?" asked Uncle Bennie, surveying his duster suspiciously.

"You know it's not," said Rachel. "It's a duster."

"Oh," said Uncle Bennie a little disconsolately.

It was very still in church, very cool and very still. They went up one pew and down the next, dusting carefully, dusting even the corners of the dark brown wooden pews. They couldn't remember exactly which pew was Mrs. Widdemeyer's so they had to dust each one carefully lest it be hers.

It was slow work and soon they felt they had been dusting for hours. Yet they were only halfway down one of the middle rows of pews. There were two wide rows of pews in the middle of the church and two narrow rows, one on each side. The bright sun outside filtered through the stained-glass windows and, in the beginning, they worked silently and solemnly. After all, this was the first time they had ever been in church unless church was going on.

Suddenly Uncle Bennie said in a very loud whisper, "Hey. This church? Where everybody?"

"Sh-sh-sh. This is church but this is Saturday," said Rachel. "Nobody is here on Saturday."

"God here?" asked Uncle Bennie.

"Yes. Only us and God."

"God everywhere," said Uncle Bennie with satisfaction. "Even on Saturday."

Once the silence had been broken by Uncle Bennie they all talked as they worked and for a time they seemed to be going very fast. How they dusted! Up one pew and down the next. It was really hard work. Jerry did not care how hard he worked though. Thoughts of the little puppy that was going to be his when the last pew and pulpit were dusted put heart and speed in his hands. In Rachel's too. But not in Uncle Bennie's. He was merely making a chivalrous gesture toward this unusual way of spending Saturday. After all, he was only three and who would expect him to take the dusting of the pews seriously? Uncle Bennie was having a good time anyway, climbing up and down the pews and pushing all the hymnals and prayer books to the ends of their little racks. They'd have to straighten these all out later, thought Jerry worriedly. And how were they ever going to finish by six o'clock?

Rachel, too, was thinking the same thing. Moreover, her arms were very tired and both she and Jerry had begun to slow up. Occasionally they looked ahead and behind to see how much ground had been covered, and how much was still to be done. There was plenty still to be done. "We should not look ahead or behind," panted Rachel. "Just keep on going."

Then Rachel had a very bright idea. Here was Uncle Bennie, she thought, only making more work for them, pushing books around. They could make use of him, she decided, and have fun besides. Mama always said, "If you can have fun doing your work, have fun." She could see no harm in that.

"Come here, Uncle Bennie," she said. "Game."

"Have fun?" asked Uncle Bennie hopefully. He was beginning to have had enough of church.

"Have plenty of fun," said Rachel. And Uncle Bennie came climbing over the pew.

Rachel had a quite long duster and she tied it

around Uncle Bennie's pants. "Whee-ee," she said, sending him sliding down the long pew.

Well. Did Uncle Bennie like that? He certainly did and now Jerry got at one end of a pew and Rachel at the other and they sent Uncle Bennie sliding back and forth across the pews. They no longer cared about the corners. They must surely have passed Mrs. Widdemeyer's pew by now, and who sat in corners anyway?

"Whee-ee," said Rachel, sending Uncle Bennie sliding down one long pew.

And, "Whee-ee," said Jerry, picking him up, putting him on the next pew, and sending him sliding back.

This was great fun for everybody and particularly for Uncle Bennie who thought it almost as good as

sledding. He did not mind at all being turned into a duster. They soon finished the long pews in this pleasant manner and started on the little side pews. When Uncle Bennie got tired of the new game, Rachel and Jerry tied the dusters around their own waists and slid back and forth across the pews themselves. Now the work went so much quicker that they finished the last pew as the clock in the other church, the little white church, on the Green, struck one, two, three, four.

The light shining through the church windows was growing dim and the children were growing very tired and hungry. There were now only the long choir stalls, two on each side, and the pulpit, and they would be finished.

"We'll save the pulpit for the end," said Rachel, having an idea the pulpit was the dessert of the job.

While they were dusting the long choir stalls, in came the altar ladies to arrange the flowers for tomorrow's service, and to polish things up at this end of the church. So the children had to take the dusters off and be businesslike. However, the altar ladies paid no attention to the pew dusters. They said not a word, quietly did their arranging, and tiptoed out.

Now. There was just one place left to dust and

this was the pulpit. "I'll dust it," said Rachel, anxious to get up in the pulpit and hoping the others did not have the same desire. They were quite content, though, to sit in the front pew and rest while Rachel did this last important dusting.

At first Rachel felt very timid about going up in the minister's pulpit, standing there, and dusting it. It was quite an awesome thing to do, stand in a minister's pulpit, the place where he delivered his sonorous sermons and read the lessons for the day. She resolved to dust it carefully by hand, so that when the Reverend Gandy was waving his arms and exhorting the congregation, the palms of his hands would not be black with dust and cause consternation among his flock.

But once Rachel was up there in the pulpit she forgot her timidity. In fact, the more she recalled how the minister looked and sounded doing his exhorting the less timid she became. In the end, she waved her duster in the air and started to exhort her congregation which, in this case, consisted of Jerry and Uncle Bennie. Uncle Bennie was beginning to look sleepy and, like tall Judge Ball and short dumpy Mrs. Widdemeyer on Sundays, he needed a bit of waking up.

Jerry and Uncle Bennie could not help laughing.

Neither one of them thought they should be laughing in church, but they couldn't help it, and naturally this inspired Rachel to more exciting and dramatic heights.

"Ca' the Ethiopia' cha'ge his ski' or the leopar' his spo'?" she demanded, remembering a story Gramma told of a certain missionary who, returning from Africa, delivered his text in this fashion, for he had some difficulty with his speech.

This doubled Uncle Bennie up with joy, for he remembered the story too. "Ca' the Ethiopia' . . ." he repeated.

"Hush," said Rachel. "Let me be the minister. And let you be the congregation." Obediently Uncle Bennie kept still, waiting for more fun. This fun Rachel was happy to supply with a rendition that was supposed to represent the Reverend Gandy when he was most eloquent.

At this triumphant moment, out of a corner of her eye, Rachel thought she glimpsed the Reverend Gandy himself, standing in one of the rear side doorways of the church. She didn't dare to take a good look to make sure. She was frozen with embarrassment, her arms raised to heaven, as still as in a painted picture. Then, with great presence of mind, she switched from her meaningless garble, her imitation of the minister, to a quiet exhortation to Jerry and Uncle Bennie to go to Sunday school, to go often, and to be good boys, and not to spend their Sunday school pennies on peanuts, but to put them in the plate.

She paused. She moved her eyes as far to their corners as she could, in order to see, without turning her head, whether or not the minister was there. She thought he was.

Jerry and Uncle Bennie laughed and laughed. They were in stitches. They didn't know that Rachel thought she saw the minister, and they laughed harder at the funny face she was making, her eye-rolling, than they had at her speech.

"Laugh not in church," counseled Rachel.

"It's a wonder something doesn't smite her down," marveled Jerry.

"Sm-i-te her down," echoed Uncle Bennie.

"Attend the Friday evening lectures on Jerusalem," suggested Rachel. "They are free. And there are colored slides," she added. "Above all, come with clean hands," she said as an afterthought.

Then, with great dignity, she backed down out of the pulpit and, wiping her brow on her duster, sat down with Jerry and Uncle Bennie.

"Hey," she whispered. "Turn around, Jerry, and see if the minister is standing in the side door."

"Jiminy crickets," muttered Jerry. He turned around but there was no one in the doorway, or in any of the doorways.

"He was there," said Rachel. "I think he was. Will I be cast out of the church?"

"Might be," said Jerry. He suddenly realized how tired he was. And here his sister was, getting herself cast out of churches on the day he was earning his dollar to buy the puppy that was over in Speedys' barn. Perhaps getting himself cast out too, and even Uncle Bennie, as partners. It would only be fair, since Rachel had helped with the dusting of the pews, to ask to be cast out of the church along with her, if she were singled out. But he was annoyed with her. Then Rachel looked so unhappy he said, "Shucks. He probably wasn't there at all. You're always thinking things."

Their work was finished and they tiptoed across the church and down the long twilit chancel to the Parish House where they left the dusters in the little closet in which they had found them. Then they went out of the Parish House door into the late-afternoon waning sunlight.

There, in the garden in front of the Parish House, was the Reverend Gandy plucking off dead chrysanthemums and withered leaves. He had his long black clericals on under his regular suit jacket. He smiled benignly at the children.

"We've been dusting the pews, sir," explained Jerry.

"Ah-h-h," said the minister. "You are the youngest pew dusters I have ever seen."

The three children smiled. Had he been standing in the doorway or hadn't he?

"Come to the lantern slides in the fall," suggested the Reverend Gandy. "They are in color."

"And free," said Uncle Bennie.

"We will, we will," cried Jerry and Rachel hastily, and they ran as fast as they could, yanking Uncle Bennie's red wagon behind them.

"We won't miss one," Rachel shouted over her shoulder to the Reverend Gandy, who nodded approvingly and then stooped to pluck a flower; and the three children dashed across the Green as the clock in the other church, the little white church, struck five.

3

The Mysterious Footsteps

Mrs. Speedy's was the last house on Elm Street on the way out to the reservoir. She owned several cows and had quite a dairy. It was far from the Green but the children could easily get there before six o'clock. Nevertheless, they ran practically all the way in order to have a little leeway. Supposing that other person, who wanted the same puppy as Jerry, should already be hanging around waving his dollar, hoping Jerry wouldn't show up? Then Mrs. Speedy might think a bird in the hand's worth two in the bush and let him have it a few minutes ahead of time.

Why had that other person picked out the same puppy as Jerry anyway, they wondered. All the puppies were very nice and when Mrs. Speedy told the person this certain brown-and-white one was promised to Jerry Pye, you would think he'd say, "OK then. I'll take this other one." But no. Jerry's puppy was the one the person wanted, according to Mrs. Speedy, and he wanted no substitute.

But Jerry forgot about the other person when they reached Mrs. Speedy's. They rushed right out to the huge barn to make sure Jerry's puppy was

still there. He was! He, and all the puppies, yapped joyously and tumbled all over one another when they saw Jerry. They recognized him because he had come to play with them nearly every day. Not having any tails left to speak of, and what little they had being bandaged up, they had to wag their whole selves in their delight.

Mrs. Speedy was at the other end of the long barn, where the cows were. A rosy light shone through the doorway from the great red disk of setting sun. Though Jerry Pye had been here often to see the puppies, this was only the second time in her life that Rachel had been inside of Speedys' barn.

The other time that Rachel had been inside of Speedys' barn was by accident, long ago, when she was about seven. She and Jerry had come over to this part of town to a big party the Sunday school teacher, Miss Foote, was giving. It was wintertime and very cold and since Miss Foote's house was on a steep slippery hill, she had said, "Bring your sleds."

It had grown dark early but this did not matter, for Japanese lanterns had been hung in the chestnut trees and made lovely colored reflections in the snow and ice. The children slid down the steep little hill that Miss Foote's house was perched on, and when

they grew cold they went indoors for hot chocolate; and then they came out to slide some more. They never wanted to go home, for none of them had ever slid downhill by the light of Japanese lanterns before.

For one slide Rachel got going with such momentum she not only slid down Miss Foote's short steep little hill, she kept right on going, and to her delight found herself sailing down a long gradual slope that seemed never to end. It was like movies of ski jumpers, she thought. On and on she went. If a prize were to have been given at this party for the longest slide she would surely have won it. When finally she stopped, she was in a big barren icy field with a few frozen spikes of last year's long grass sticking up here and there out of the snow. It was dark and there were no Japanese lanterns and no other children nearby sliding. Then suddenly she knew she was lost in the big dark ice field and she didn't know the way back.

Rachel looked all around and before she had time to get frightened she saw a light twinkling, a dark red light. She thought it might be one of the Japanese lanterns, though how it had got way over here, all by itself, she did not understand. But it was reassuring to see it and she made her way toward it. The light turned out to be in Speedys' barn. Mrs. Speedy was milking the cows by the light of a dark red lantern which was what Rachel had seen. Stepping into the barn was like stepping into a painting, a painting that was dark excepting where the red cows were, and Mrs. Speedy's ruddy face, the lantern, and the white milk that looked purple. Although Rachel had never been inside this place before, she had passed it from the outside, going up Shingle Hill on picnics. So she had figured in a second what place she was in. It was like waking from a dream to find herself this far from the party, like being in a surprising new world. But it was a relief to be somewhere and not sliding around in the bare empty field.

Instead of trying to find the party again Rachel had run as fast as she could all the way to the Green, her sled bobbing along behind her and knocking into her heels, and then all the way home.

Jerry had come home soon afterwards. No one at the party had missed her, not even Jerry. Rachel didn't tell anyone about being in the picture of Speedys' barn because it was a hard thing to explain. But it was interesting to remember, as she was doing now.

Today it was a little lighter in the barn than it

had been that other time, for this was still summer. But the same dusty red lantern hung from a rafter and the cows were down at the other end of the barn, and again it was like being in a painting.

Mrs. Speedy waved to the children and soon came over to them. "Well," she said. "I suppose you have come for your puppy?"

"Yes," said Jerry proudly.

"He's a fine dog, you bet," said Mrs. Speedy.

"Yes," said Jerry. "Here's the dollar," he said.

So Mrs. Speedy took the dollar and Jerry tenderly picked up his puppy, his own puppy, his little brown-and-white dog. The children were beside themselves with joy. Here they had this real live puppy, it was theirs, their very own real, honest-to-goodness dog, and nobody else's. Jerry let Rachel hold him sometimes because she had helped with the dusting, and also Uncle Bennie, showing him how to pat the puppy and not squeeze him. They just loved him, they did.

As they left Speedys' barn Jerry happened to glimpse someone racing across the fields behind the dairy, leaping over the old telephone poles lying there. Jerry didn't pay much attention to the person because he was so excited about having his own puppy in his arms at last. Anyway there were dark shadows in the fields now and the only thing about the leaping person he got any impression of was his hat. It was a sort of yellow-mustard-colored hat.

Must be someone getting some milk, he thought and soon forgot about the person. Jerry did not connect this person with that other person who had been trying to buy his dog. Naturally, he would expect a person who was planning to do something as important as buy a dog to approach the house from the front way, and not be coming leaping over telephone poles and brooks and skunk cabbages to get there.

"What kind of a dog is he?" asked Rachel, this being her turn to hold the puppy a minute. "Did you say he is a fox terrier?"

"Yes. He's purebred, part fox terrier and part collie. There may also be a little bull in him too," boasted Jerry.

They were so pleased with, and interested in, the puppy they dragged Uncle Bennie all the long way to his home without noticing the distance at all. Rachel and Jerry could hardly eat one bite of the supper Gramma had prepared for them and they had no idea what they were eating until they reached the dessert. Then they knew that what they were eating was some of Gramma's homemade peach ice cream because of hard pieces of frozen peach that hurt their teeth.

Usually Gramma urged them to eat more, more

of everything. "Eat more rolls," she'd say, when they had already eaten so many of her tiny delicious hot little rolls they didn't see how they could possibly swallow another one. Still they would always find space because Gramma would be hurt if they did not eat just one more and just one more. But tonight Gramma could see they were in a hurry to get home to show Mama their fine dog, so she only urged them once or twice, instead of her usual dozen times, to have more ice cream.

Gramma was very pleased that Uncle Bennie had spent the afternoon dusting the pews. "He may be a minister when he grows up," she said.

Uncle Bennie did not want them to leave with the puppy. But when Rachel and Jerry assured him he would see the puppy next Saturday, and every Saturday, he felt better. Anyway, he was awfully tired and sleepy and he sat down in the doorway, grabbing hold of his old bubbah, tickling his nose with it, sucking his thumb, and blinking his eyes drowsily.

Uncle Bennie called not only his old pink blanket "bubbah," he called the little bits of wool he plucked from it and with which he tickled his nose and chin and even his knees "bubbah," too. When he waked up in the morning the first thing he would say, ecstatically, was, "Ah-h. Bubbah!" Sometimes he would crawl around on his hands and knees picking up old stray pieces of bubbah he had dropped. And, outdoors, he might find a little speck that Gramma had shaken from the rugs. "Ah-h, Bubbah!" he would exclaim and gather it fondly up.

There had been a time when he plucked the wool not only off his old pink blanket, his *real* bubbah, but off the camel's-hair rugs from the Orient also. Gramma finally had to store these rugs away before they should disappear in thin air. She bade Uncle Bennie to be economical, to save his bubbah, and use only the little bits he found here and there instead of always plucking new bits to tickle his nose. She said, "Bubbah will wear out and then you will not have Bubbah anymore."

But Uncle Bennie was spendthrift. He did not look to the future, and he still plucked at his bubbah and tickled his nose with it. But he had agreed to leave it home and not take it with him anymore, now he was a big boy of three.

So now Bubbah made up to Uncle Bennie for the departure of the puppy and Jerry and Rachel, and he solemnly, tickling his nose, watched them prepare to leave.

"We'll see you next week," Rachel called to him.

"Go church again?" asked Uncle Bennie.

"Maybe."

"See puppy again?"

"Sure. He's our puppy now."

" 'Bye."

" 'Bye."

By the time Rachel and Jerry started on the long way home, way over on the other side of town, it had grown dark. Whenever they came to a street-lamp they put the little dog down so he could stretch his legs, and they kept exclaiming over all the wonderful things about him—his ears, his eyes, his softness, his roundness, his whole self. The puppy did not seem to miss his life in the barn at all. He was happy to belong to Jerry and Rachel and he kept frisking about.

"He likes me," said Jerry happily.

"Oh-h. Isn't he cunning!" admired Rachel.

"And smart, too. He's going to do tricks. I'll teach him everything," said Jerry proudly.

"Gracie can open the front door," Rachel reminded Jerry. It was true. Gracie could leap in the air and turn the doorknob and, as she came down, let her weight fall against the door in such a way the door would fly open. It was a very smart thing to do, and far more pleasant to hear about than catching rats for Mama.

"Yes, Gracie's smart," agreed Jerry. "But this dog can go everywhere with me."

"Yes," said Rachel. And they walked along happily and silently.

Suddenly, Jerry realized that he heard footsteps behind him, that, furthermore, he had been hearing these footsteps for some time and thinking nothing of them. Only now did he realize that someone was following them.

It had grown very dark, especially under the great elm trees that arched Second Avenue, the street they were now on. Whenever Jerry turned around to see who, if anyone, was following them, he could see no one. The street was not a straight one. It curved and twisted, and he couldn't see far enough back to make out anything. When he and Rachel were walking, however, he was certain he could hear the footsteps behind them. When he and Rachel stopped, the footsteps stopped.

Shucks, said Jerry to himself. *I'm as bad as Rachel, always thinking things.* But he no longer put the puppy down on the ground. "It's getting awfully late," he said to Rachel. "We better hurry home or Mama will be wondering where we are."

"M-m-m," said Rachel absentmindedly.

Now Rachel had been hearing the footsteps, too.

But she had said nothing because Jerry always thought she was imagining things. She didn't think she was imagining these footsteps though she certainly hoped she was. If there were real footsteps behind them, walking when they walked, stopping when they stopped, why she and Jerry didn't just sprint for home was more than she could tell. Jerry probably had not heard them, that was why. They probably weren't there.

Meanwhile Jerry was saying to himself, "I have to see who this is that's following us. I bet it's that stranger fellow, the one who wanted to buy my puppy. And I bet it was him racing across the telephone poles in back of Speedys' barn and not someone after milk. Maybe it was even him, and not the minister, Rachel saw in the doorway of the church when she was being a minister in the pulpit."

He decided that at the next street corner where there was a good bright light they would wait and let the coward get past them. He wanted to tell Rachel they were being followed, but she would probably get so scared she'd yell, and then he wouldn't ever see what the person looked like. Jerry didn't know why he was so certain that the person behind them was the same person that wanted his puppy, too. But he was. His heart pounded. The fellow better not try and take this dog away from him that he had bought just a little while ago from Mrs. Speedy for one dollar, that he and Rachel and Uncle Bennie had earned dusting the pews for tall Sam Doody. He better not.

When they reached the brightly lighted corner of Spruce and Second Avenue, Jerry stopped suddenly, grabbing Rachel's arm to make her stop short in her tracks, too. As clear as thunder they heard the footsteps and then they heard them stop short, too.

Still Rachel said nothing. She was not going to be told she was hearing things. But Jerry said, "You hear that?"

"Yes," said Rachel.

"Somebody's been following us."

"Yes. All the way from Gramma's."

"Yes. And I think this person was at Speedys' barn when we were there and probably followed us to Gramma's. And hung around there until we left. He's after my dog, that's what."

"Hung around in the dark," said Rachel, her spine prickling a little, to tell the truth, though here they were in their own town of Cranbury where they knew every street and lane and practically all the people. Moreover, here they were now, under a huge purple streetlight and outside the house of Judge Ball whose pew they had just dusted, though he didn't know it. And who could do them any harm or snatch their dog away? No one. Pooh!

"We'll just sit here on the curb under this bright light until whoever it is comes along. When he does come we can run up on Judge Ball's front porch. He wouldn't mind. And if he doesn't come, and is just waiting for us to get going again so he can follow us some more, we just won't move. We won't move until somebody else comes by that we can walk along with and be safe."

This was a very sensible plan and the two children sat down on the curb to wait. Jerry put his sleepy puppy inside his blouse because the evenings were getting cooler and he didn't want his puppy ever catching cold or anything. It felt wonderful having the warm little animal against his heart. He could even feel the puppy's fast little heartbeat against his.

Jiminy crickets, he thought. *I got a real dog now.*

While they were sitting still on the curb, they heard nothing—no footsteps, no stifled coughs or sneezes as in mystery stories, nothing. They wanted to get home. Maybe they had both been imagining things.

"Oh, come on," said Jerry impatiently. "Let's go."

They left the bright streetlight and they started down the dark tree-rustling street. No one was around for it was suppertime. They could smell different cooking smells as they passed each house. In one they were having pork chops, and in others they heard the clatter of dishes being washed in the kitchen.

"Do you hear them now, the footsteps?" whispered Rachel.

"Sh-sh-sh. No," said Jerry.

They began to run and they made so much noise clattering up the sidewalk they couldn't hear anything but themselves anymore. They ran for a whole block and now there were just two long blocks to their home on Beam's Place. They stopped to catch their breath. They listened, trying to hear footsteps above their panting. They did hear them. It was spooky.

"Jiminy crickets," gulped Jerry.

Then they had another piece of luck. Sam Doody, with a big suit box in his hand, came striding up the street, on his way home from town. He had got off the new Second Avenue trolley car. This was the second time in one day that Sam Doody had saved them; first—the dollar for dusting the pews that enabled them to buy their puppy, and now—here he was, saving them from the unknown footstepper, as Rachel had nicknamed the person in her mind already. Sam Doody lived only a few doors from them and he didn't mind at all their tagging right along with him.

"Well," he said, grinning. "Dust the pews?"

"Yes," said Jerry. "We dusted them good. The pulpit too. Everything."

"Fine," said Sam Doody. "You saved my life."

"You saved ours," said Jerry.

"We got a dog," said Rachel.

Jerry opened up his blouse and let Sam Doody take a look and touch his puppy. While they were all standing outside of Sam Doody's house, with Sam Doody admiring the puppy properly, Jerry and Rachel thought they heard the footsteps again. But they didn't care because tall Sam Doody was there and he was the captain of the basketball team. Moreover they were only two doors from home.

"S'long," said Sam.

"S'long," said Jerry and Rachel; and they made a dash for their own front door.

They rushed in and they went into their dark little parlor and, lifting the stiff net curtains, they looked out. They saw a person glide behind their big horse chestnut tree! And they saw this dark shadowy figure move off up the street.

"Did you see his hat?" asked Jerry.

"Not good," said Rachel. "It looked sort of orange or yellow. A funny color."

"Same man," said Jerry with satisfaction. At least he knew what the stranger's hat looked like. At least he knew that much. And he told Rachel about the person leaping across the telephone poles up at Speedys'. Now that he recalled that scene, it seemed as though the person had been sort of crouching as he leaped. "Sneaky, like," he told Rachel. And he suggested also that maybe it had been this man with the hat that Rachel thought she had seen in the doorway of the church, and not the Reverend Gandy.

"Oh-h," gasped Rachel, there being so many developments to take in. She certainly hoped it had been the minister and not the man with the hat. She

would rather be cast out of church, she thought, than to have had the man with the hat snooping on them that long!

"How'd you know it was a man?" asked Rachel.

"Man's hat," said Jerry.

"Oh, of course," said Rachel.

"Beats me," said Jerry. "If he wanted to grab the puppy, why didn't he? He had plenty of chance all the long way home."

"Um-m-m," said Rachel, puzzled. "Maybe he just wanted to see where we live."

"Jiminy. We should have doubled on our tracks and thrown him off," said Jerry.

"We didn't though. Here we are and now he knows where we live. Do you think he would steal the puppy sometime?"

"No. We'll always be with the puppy."

"School starts Tuesday."

"We'll tell Mama never to let him out of the yard. But we're dumbbells. We should have thrown him off our trail somehow."

"It happened so suddenly we didn't have time to think," said Rachel consolingly.

"Yes, but we're dumbbells. Tomorrow I'll ask Mrs. Speedy, you bet, who the other person was that wanted our puppy, so's we'll know who to watch out for."

"Um-m-m. Besides the hat."

Later they told Mama about the footsteps. The story did not sound sensible anymore. Maybe they had really imagined the whole business. Mama didn't seem to be paying much attention to the story of the "mysterious footstepper," or the "man with the hat," as the stranger was called by Rachel and Jerry. But that night she locked the doors extra carefully. "We don't want any unsavory characters roaming around," she said.

Mama liked the puppy. They all liked him. Gracie-the-cat had gone out for her night prowling. She was not yet introduced.

4

The Naming of Ginger Pye

Gracie-the-cat took an immediate liking to the new
member of the family. She was not at all jealous.
After her first long incredulous stare when they were
introduced the next morning, she tried to give the
puppy a good washing. He accepted a lick or two
but he would not stay still long enough for more and
made a game of it. When he got too impudent Gracie
gave him a cuffing, but she kept her claws in. And
if he came pouncing on her during her nap she spit
at him. But, all in all, her feelings toward the puppy
were tolerant and kindly.

In the bright light of morning it seemed nonsense
to even remember about the mysterious footstepper.
Nevertheless, Jerry rushed over to Mrs. Speedy's
the first thing in the morning to find out who the
fellow was who had also wanted to buy his dog. He
wanted some idea, besides a hat, as to whom to be

on guard against. But instead of Mrs. Speedy leading the cows to pasture, he found Mr. Speedy.

Mr. Speedy said Mrs. Speedy had been struck in the night with a stroke and would be in the hospital for some time. Mr. Speedy was not the friendly type. He did not like children standing around watching him milk or churn or mow. Anyway, with Mrs. Speedy being sick, Jerry could not ask him if Mrs. Speedy had ever told him the odd thing of two people wanting the same puppy, Jerry being the one, and the other being the mystery. So he raced back home, knowing nothing.

This was Sunday and everyone was so interested in watching the puppy it was hard to do anything else. Rachel and Jerry were allowed to stay home from Sunday school this once, to play with the puppy. After all, they had spent yesterday in church— dusting pews, to be sure—but still in church.

Rachel appreciated the permission to stay home. However, she thought she'd better go to Sunday school anyway in case it had been the minister who had stood in the doorway yesterday while she was dusting the pulpit, and not the mysterious footstepper. She was almost certain, no matter what Jerry thought, that it had been the minister. How would the footstepper ever have known she and Jerry were

in church anyway? She didn't want to be cast out of the church for acting like a minister in a pulpit and she imagined that perfect attendance at Sunday school would lessen that likelihood.

She bade a reluctant farewell to her family and the new puppy and arrived at Sunday school just as church, which came first, was letting out. Mr. Gandy was standing in the doorway shaking hands with all the people. The organ was still pealing joyously, and Rachel stood watching the congregation pour out and stream across the Green. It was remarkable how differently she felt toward her church and the congregation now she had dusted the pews. She didn't feel like the minister, exactly. But she felt a rather protective fondness for the church. It would have pleased her to stand by the minister in the doorway and shake the hands of those he missed.

Had people noticed the special dusting the pews had had? Rachel wondered. She examined the back of Mrs. Widdemeyer's white cotton embroidered dress to see if there was any dust on it and there wasn't. She couldn't understand why they had to be so careful of Mrs. Widdemeyer's pew because Mrs. Widdemeyer always brought one of her husband's big white handkerchiefs along with her and spread it out on the pew before sitting down. You would think

they could skip dusting her part of the pew altogether, and likewise Judge Ball's, for he did the
same with his handkerchief, not caring to get a speck
on his black suit.

Tall Sam Doody came grinning out of church
with a dark blue-purple suit on. It was not anyway
near as splendid a suit as the dark green one he
had had first, but naturally Rachel would not tell
him this.

At last she went into the Parish House, wondering who had dusted it, and sat down in Miss
Foote's class which was just coming to order. To
counteract her behavior in the pulpit Rachel intended to make a good impression on the Sunday
school teacher. But Miss Foote kept telling her please
not to fidget so. The truth was Rachel could not take
her mind off the puppy any longer and she was
anxious to get home and see what cute thing he was
doing now. Moreover, she had given the minister a
good chance to cast her out if he wanted to cast her
out. She had stood right in front of him, practically
inviting him to cast her out. Yet he had not done
so. The chances were he was not ever going to do
so. So now, she might as well go home and see the
puppy.

The puppy! Goodness, they had forgotten to name

him so far. They just called him "pup, pup." A dog couldn't go through life just being called "pup, pup." Supposing Uncle Bennie had never been given a name, but was called "baby, baby," all the time. It would be the same thing and all wrong. When finally Sunday school was let out, a little earlier than usual because a thunderstorm was coming up, she rushed home under the darkening sky. Supposing they had named the puppy while she was at Sunday school and she had been left out of the naming?

"What are we going to name him?" she asked, bursting into the house.

To her surprise Uncle Bennie was there. He had not been able to wait until next Saturday to see the puppy again, and Gramma had had to bring him over in his Sunday clothes. Mama hadn't got the dinner ready yet, she had been so interested in the puppy. Now she dropped the potato she was peeling and looked at the children in surprise. "Why," she said. "Mean to say you haven't named him yet?"

Jerry felt ashamed. He had been so happy just having this dog he hadn't even thought of naming him. Now he thought hard, however. He thought of all the names of dogs he knew. They were Duke, Major, Rex, Queenie, Lassie, Lad, and Tige. He liked the name of Duke best. But that was the name of the big hound of his friend, Dick Badger, the hound that could scratch his stomach when you scratched his back. It was a very funny thing to watch. But this puppy of his was going to be funnier. This puppy of his. What would they name him? Naturally there could not be two Dukes in the same block.

"Aren't you thinking?" he asked Rachel.

"I am thinking. But I haven't thought of anything good enough yet."

"Well, think harder," said Jerry, while their puppy came racing through the house with a big fuzzy orange woolly duster he had found early and appropriated for himself. There he stood, in the doorway of the kitchen with his duster in his mouth, ready to tear off again. "Catch me if you can," he seemed to say, taunting them, daring them to come, exceedingly impudent.

"Woof!" he barked, dropping the duster.

Jerry grabbed the handle end of the duster and the puppy buried his nose in the wool end and worried it and shook it and growled and snorted. He was having a wonderful time and so were all of them. Jerry held the duster high in the air and the puppy hung on to it with his strong little teeth and swung. Uncle Bennie kept leaping up and down and

yelling, "Hey! Hey!" Thunder began to rumble, adding to the general confusion. The kitchen grew dark and Mama had to light the gas mantle.

"At this rate, when will I ever get dinner ready?" Mama wondered.

But the children hadn't even thought yet how hungry they were. They were too busy chasing the puppy and thinking of names.

"How about calling him 'Frisco' because he is so frisky?" asked Jerry doubtfully, not at all sure this was a good name.

"Um-m-m," they all said hesitantly.

"What about 'Boombernickles'?" asked Rachel.

"Oh, Rachel," said Jerry in disgust. He was not always as careful about not hurting her feelings as she was his.

"I was just joking," said Rachel quickly.

Uncle Bennie said, "Call puppy 'Bumpy'?"

"Why 'Bumpy'?" they asked.

"Bumps into everything, he goes so fast," said Uncle Bennie.

This sounded like a very good name, but Jerry was not completely satisfied. It was the best so far, however. Then Mama said, "Well, he looks like ginger, and he acts like ginger. Why not call him 'Ginger'?"

"Ginger," they all repeated dubiously. None of them could think of anything better though and so they called this dog "Ginger," and it went well with Pye. Ginger Pye.

"People will think it is Gingerbread. And all the while it will be Ginger Pye," said Rachel who liked reasonableness.

Rachel's reasonableness was not always easy for Jerry to agree with. There was quite often likely to be a catch to it. For instance, there was the time of the poison tomatoes. That time he and Rachel had been sitting on the back fence, just talking and thinking. They looked down into the yard behind them which was overgrown with weeds, for the people were away for the summer. Yet amidst the rampant weeds a few sad-looking tomato plants were growing. And through the weeds and plants Rachel had spotted three beautiful ripe red tomatoes. It was a marvel they could have grown so perfect with all the weeds and burrs smothering them. But they had, and Jerry's mouth drooled hungrily, even now, recollecting them.

He had jumped over the fence and picked them and climbed back up, and he had been all set to put his teeth in his when Rachel had shouted at him, so loud he nearly fell off the fence. "Stop,"

she had yelled. "Don't eat them," she had said.
"They're poison," she had explained.

"Poison!" he had said.

"Yes, poison," she had said. And she explained
that though the people were away and the tomatoes
would go to rot, still they could not eat them because
in the first place that would be stealing. And in the
second place they were poison anyway, and they
would die if they did. The stealing reason Jerry had
discarded because he knew the neighbors well and
they would not have minded their tomatoes being
eaten. In fact, they would have liked to think they

were not going to waste. The poison was another matter.

Where had Rachel got the theory the tomatoes were poison, he had asked her impatiently. She had got the theory, she said, from a story she had just a few minutes before finished reading. This story was in a little booklet the Corn Fluffies people had sent out. In the story some children, who were supposed not to eat some certain fruit because it was poisoned, *had* eaten the fruit and become quite sick. If they had stuck to Corn Fluffies they would not have become sick. Now these tomatoes, she said, were in the same category. They were poison. Why else would they be growing down there amidst the burrs? Anyway, she talked so persuasively she had Jerry convinced. And not only would she not let Jerry eat the tomatoes, she made him bury them deep in the earth of the lot across the street so the poison would not spread and spread all over the earth like the poison in the broken mirror in the story of *The Snow Queen*.

"That is all book stuff," Jerry had reasoned ruefully after it was all over and Rachel had skipped off with Addie Egan. "And why do I ever, ever listen to her?" he had asked himself, half of a mind to go back and dig the tomatoes up again. But why take a chance with poison?

The poison tomatoes showed, though, exactly how unreasonable Rachel's reasonableness could be. When she did her most earnest talking was when you had to watch out. Was there a catch now to this Ginger Pye, Gingerbread business? Jerry couldn't see a catch to it. So he said happily, "Ginger is sort of a good name for him, isn't it? Sort of a just right name? We'll call the puppy Ginger. All right."

"Ginger Pye, not Gingerbread," murmured Rachel dreamily.

Ginger, who did not seem to care what he was named, or that he had been named, had fallen asleep under the kitchen table with one paw stretched in a proprietary fashion over his duster. He did not seem to mind the slashes of lightning or the rumbling thunder at all. Perhaps this was because he was used to the lowing and the mooing of the cows in Speedys' barn.

It was certainly good he was not like a big collie dog Jerry knew, named Lassie, who had to be locked in a closet during thunderstorms. Otherwise she would manage to get out of the house and run around like mad in the rain, not remembering where she lived or who she was or anything. Ginger, on the contrary, slept as peacefully through the storm as if it were a lullaby.

Since Ginger was now asleep, and since Mama would not let Uncle Bennie wake him up, saying, "Let the poor little thing rest awhile," and since dinner was still not ready, Jerry and Uncle Bennie went down cellar to hammer and pound. Mama was busy stirring the food in the pots and pans and the kitchen smelled as though they were going to have roast lamb. Rachel set the table, in the kitchen, because Papa was still away. Even though it was Sunday they always ate in the kitchen when Papa was away, saving a lot of time and steps. Then Rachel went into the living room to wait for dinner which smelled unbearably good.

It was a terrific thunderstorm, but once it got started it was over in ten minutes. The thunder had boomed, the lightning sizzled, the rain splashed down, horse chestnuts had fallen from the tree, and the birds were silent. When it was over Rachel felt as though the world had been born anew. She had spent these ten minutes of big storm in the big armchair doing nothing but appreciating the storm. When no more rain was falling, except big drops pelting slowly from the horse chestnut tree and the roof, she returned to the kitchen. Would dinner ever be ready? she wondered.

That was what Jerry and Uncle Bennie were

wondering, too. And they pushed open the cellar door looking grimy as stokers on a ship, and almost starved. Jerry listened. "The storm is now three miles away," he said, counting between the flashes of lightning and the lazy thunder.

"Three miles," echoed Uncle Bennie, admiring Jerry's knowledge.

They all sat down to dinner which, at last, was ready. Ginger waked up and came and ate his dinner under a little settee beneath the kitchen window.

"Ah, Ginger. Ginger Pye," said Rachel affectionately, making a loving face at him as one does to babies.

Ginger. Ginger Pye, thought Jerry. The name did sound good, the way Rachel said it.

During this whole day so far there had been no sign of the mysterious footstepper, the man with the muddy mustard hat. Dinner was still going on. They were up to the dessert—Jell-O and sliced bananas with powdered sugar sprinkled on top. Uncle Bennie was sitting in Rachel's old high chair and, from it, he could see out of the little window over the sink better than the others could. All of a sudden he said, "I see hot! I see hot!"

"Hot" was the way Uncle Bennie always pronounced "hat." Forgetting this and thinking he was just remarking on the food, at first no one paid any attention to him. But since he continued to point out the little window over the sink and exclaim, "Hot! Hot!" it suddenly dawned on Jerry that maybe it was *the* hat, the odd yellow hat, that Uncle Bennie was talking about.

Jerry ran to the window. It was! There was a queer yellow sort of a hat just like the one he had seen on the person racing across the fields at Mrs. Speedy's, and it looked as though it was glued to the side fence. The person must be looking through a knothole. If Jerry got out there fast enough he would see who this was, anyway. He tore out of the house, followed by Rachel and Mama, who grabbed Uncle Bennie out of his high chair. But by the time Jerry got to the fence and climbed up it, the snooper had disappeared. Jerry jumped down and raced to the corner but then he didn't know which way to turn. There was no trace of anyone, anywhere. If Jerry hadn't seen the hat, too, he would have thought Uncle Bennie had made it up.

Reluctantly he returned home and he looked through the knothole the man with the hat had been looking through. He would nail it up.

"Did you see anything of the man but his hat?" Jerry asked Uncle Bennie. It really would not have

made any difference if Uncle Bennie had seen the entire person for all men grown-ups looked alike to him, and all lady grown-ups looked alike. Only children looked different from one another to him.

"Just saw hot," said Uncle Bennie.

So they still knew nothing more about the unsavory character than they had before, except that he had become a very real person whom the Pyes had to watch out for.

Unsavory character. It sounded like a name. "Unsavory could be his first name. And Character his last," suggested Rachel. "Like in colonial times. It sounds like those names."

"M-m-m," said Jerry.

Why did that person persist in thinking he could get hold of their puppy? Ginger belonged to the Pyes. He already had a name, Ginger Pye, and he already had a little leather collar around his neck made out of one of Rachel's old skate straps. Anyone could see he really belonged. As soon as he was old enough they would get a license for him. And to keep him safe and sound, they wouldn't let him out of the backyard by himself until he was old enough to bark like the dickens, and even bite, if anybody tried to make off with him.

Moreover, if Unsavory continued to snoop around

they could tell the policeman. They could describe his hat and the policeman would catch him. Let the man watch out, or he would land in jail, the Cranbury jail, where no one had landed in ten years.

That was the way the Pyes were talking as they went into the house and made sure the doors were latched. Who latched doors in Cranbury in the daytime, if they were at home? Maybe Judge Ball. Hardly anyone else, though. But the Pyes latched theirs today all right, in case Unsavory should come back. However, they didn't see any more of him or his hat that day.

5

The Perpendicular Swimmer

The next day was Labor Day. When that was over, school would begin. "Hey," said Jerry Pye to his friend, Dick Badger. "Let's go up to the reservoy for one more last good swim."

It was a fine warm day and Dick said, "Sure."

Dick Badger was the boy next door who owned the big black-and-gray hound that scratched his stomach when you scratched his back. Dick Badger knew more ways of earning a nickel than anyone Jerry had ever heard of. He charged a nickel if a boy or a girl wanted to hold his kite or to scratch Duke's back. Of course he didn't charge his best friend, Jerry Pye, anything, or even Rachel or Uncle Bennie. But he charged everybody else and he always had peanuts or gumdrops in his pocket.

Dick Badger was known as the "perpendicular swimmer." That was his nickname and the way he came to be known as the perpendicular swimmer was because he almost always swam down and up, and almost never along the surface of the water the way the other fellows did.

He had learned to swim underwater before he had learned top-of-the-water swimming. He began in fairly shallow water, walking along the bottom of the sea on his hands. Before he knew it, he would be in deep water and swimming down there. Then he would have to shoot upwards for air. The reason for this underwater swimming was that he liked to feel land under his hands, even though it was wet land and at the bottom of the sea, because he felt safer. In this way he had developed his fondness for perpendicular swimming.

Of course, now he was an excellent swimmer on top of the water as well as underneath, but one rarely saw him on top except every half minute or so when he stuck his wet red nose up for air. He liked to throw shells or pebbles into the water and then swim straight down after them. He said he aimed to swim straight down to the bottom of the reservoir because he wanted to see what was down there. He had heard there was a dead cow and he wanted to see. In the ocean, likewise, he swam under the water instead of along the top. He liked it down there with the

crabs and killifish. "You should see all the killies down there today," he'd say.

Dick was a thin wiry sort of boy. On fine days, when the water was sunny and clear, it was a very pleasant sight to see him go diving down, down, and swim awhile along the pebbly bottom of the reservoir, or the sandy bottom of the salt sea, and then shoot straight upwards again in his perpendicular fashion.

Everyone admired Dick for his special kind of swimming. But sometimes the other fellows would tire of trying to keep up with him under the water and would challenge him to a race on top of the sea. This he always good-naturedly consented to do. He would always start out with the others. But then, instead of dashing straight ahead for the goal—a buoy or a lobster pot—down he would shoot, down down down. He would come back up, laughing and gasping, just about when the others would be returning to the raft or rock from the race. This perpendicular swimming did not count as winning the top-of-the-water race. However, it did excite a great deal of admiration and Dick certainly held all records for it.

Of all those who admired Dick Badger for his perpendicular swimming, naturally Jerry, being his best friend, admired him the most. And he admired his friend's big lanky dog, Duke, too, and liked to tickle his back to make him scratch his stomach. He appreciated the fact that he did not have to pay a nickel for this favor. Ginger was going to know a great many more tricks than that one. He was still just a tiny puppy. His tail wasn't completely healed although the bandage was off, and they had had him only since the day before yesterday at six o'clock. Yet he could already catch things in his mouth! Soon, he would know everything.

"I'll take Ginger pup," said Jerry proudly.

"Sure," said Dick. "Maybe he'll like a little swim."

"We can't let him in the water yet, he's too little. And I'll have to carry him most of the way," said Jerry fondly.

"Sure," said Dick.

"Rachel wants to come. OK?"

"Sure," said Dick. "She can watch Ginger while we're swimming so he doesn't get lost or drowned."

"Or so the unsavory character doesn't get him."

"Sure," said Dick. He had been told about the hat, the footsteps, the unsavory character, and he was very impressed with the mysterious aspect of the whole affair. "Uncle Bennie coming, too?" he asked.

"No. This ain't Saturday."

"Nope," said Dick.

"Rachel's got bee-bite."

"Got what?"

"Got bee-bite. 'T's getting better though."

"Sure," said Dick Badger.

Just then Rachel ran up. She was holding a damp handkerchief over her mouth. "I have bee-bite," she said importantly.

In the middle of the night Rachel had waked up thinking, *what's the matter with my lip?* It felt as though someone had put a mud pie on it. She put her finger on her lower lip and touched it carefully. It was enormous. It didn't feel like a lip at all anymore. With her tongue she couldn't feel the end of it. Moreover her lip seemed to be getting bigger and bigger all the time instead of snapping back to normal as it would have had all this been a dream. What had happened? She had had a dreadful transformation in the night. Should she wake Mama up? Mama might not recognize her.

Was she under a spell, she wondered, as in the fairy tales? There was a maiden in one fairy tale who had had a spell cast on her and her lips stuck way way out just like this. For a time Rachel lay in bed and shuddered and waited for the next awful metamorphosis, a hand changed into a bird's claw, for example.

Then dawn began to come. A light the color of robins' eggs filled the sky. Rachel stole out of bed, trying to keep it and the floor from creaking and waking the household. Mustering all her courage she looked at herself in the mirror of her little blue chiffonier. She could not help gasping. How dreadful! Her lower lip had swelled way way out and she looked like the old witch in *The Tinder Box*. Even as she looked her lip seemed to be ballooning out. Supposing it never stopped ballooning? If it got any bigger she would have to employ a sling to hold it up. She surveyed herself in utter dismay. And school! School began tomorrow. What would they do with her in school? And who would stick up for her, the way she stuck up for Addie Egan?

"Ubangi," she murmured, thinking of the pictures in the books at the library. Might she be packed off to the Ubangis to live? Thoughts of the Ubangis, the ugly old witch, and the enchanted maidens in fairy tales sent her flying at last into Mama's room. So far she had not cried, but she almost cried in relief when Mama said, "Bee-bite. That's what it is."

"Will it ever go away?" Rachel asked, confiding her fears about being like the girl in the fairy tale with the long long lip.

"Oh, yes." Mama laughed. "We'll start right now fixing up that lip."

So all morning Rachel had been bathing her lower lip in something soothing that Mama had prepared. Now it was halfway back to normal. It still felt heavy, but the fact that it was swelling down, not up, was encouraging, to say the least.

Now Rachel had a little bottle of the wash in her hands because she was to keep bathing her lip even though she was going up to the reservoir with the boys. And she was not to go in swimming because of her lip and she was to sit in the shade and mind Ginger while Jerry swam.

It was a long walk to the reservoir. The way led past Speedys' barn, past the last houses straggling up the hills, past the old red mill, and, finally,

through a narrow wooded wagon road until there they were at last—at the reservoir! In the middle of the pond the water sparkled in the sunlight, and at the edges where trees and bushes hung low over the water there were lovely shadows.

The children came out of the woods where a little dam separated the upper reservoir from the lower, and a waterfall tumbled over it. In the spring they could not cross the reservoir this way for there would be a regular Niagara here, the water roaring and tearing over the dam. Then they would have to go way around the reservoir to get to the other side. But this was the end of summer and there had not been much rain. The water was not very deep on the dam and the current not swift at all. So they took off their shoes and stockings and waded across the cool brick dam to the far side.

They stopped at their favorite rock, a large flat gray one, that was half in the shade and half out of it and from which Rachel could dangle her legs into the water if she wanted to. Jerry and Dick Badger had their swimming trunks on under their clothes. They lost no time in stripping off their shirts and pants, and into the water they went. Big lumbering Duke went in, too, making a terrible splash and he swam around with the boys for a time, bringing them sticks to throw. But when Dick began his usual underwater swimming, Duke climbed out of the reservoir and sniffed off into the woods to chase whatever small animals he could find.

Ginger was so excited over seeing all this huge lot of water he kept barking and yapping and whining and quivering the nerves on his legs and forehead. It was all Rachel could do to keep him from jumping in. But after a while he contented himself with nosing acorns about on the rock. Rachel kept soaking her swollen lip and occasionally she studied her reflection in the pond. To her great relief she saw that the swelling was disappearing and by tomorrow it would probably be all right, as Mama said.

By now Ginger was tuckered out and he lay contentedly in Rachel's lap. Sometimes he dozed and sometimes he watched the boys swim, and whenever he heard Jerry's voice his little bit of tail wagged joyously.

Up here at the reservoir it was still and beautiful. Little could be heard but the twittering of birds and the splashing and shouts of the boys. No one else was up here today except, on the far side, a man in blue, sitting on a rock. From here it looked as though he was painting a picture. On his side of the reservoir, for just a few yards, the shining tracks of the railroad could be seen, and occasionally a train shot by, leaving its trail of white smoke coiling low over the trees.

Rachel had often come to the reservoir with Papa. He liked to come here on quiet Sundays to listen to the birds and watch them. He wouldn't move a muscle and neither would she. And they would see the interesting things the birds did without the birds paying them the slightest attention. Rachel thought of all the smart birds she had ever known; especially she thought of some certain smart sparrows she had seen one day last May.

That day she had been sitting on the little top porch smelling all the flowering fruit trees and thinking, "This is spring!" Then she heard such a twittering down below she looked over the railing and what she saw was a very busy little sparrow. He was terribly excited about a piece of white tissue paper crumpled into a soft bunch that lay on the lawn. He pecked at it and stalked around it and now and then he looked quizzically up at the eaves of Dick Badger's barn. Dick's barn, which had once been a stable, was built right close to the sidewalk between his house and the Pyes. The sparrow kept chattering very noisily but finally he got this big piece of tissue paper in his mouth and flew up to the corner eave of Dick's barn.

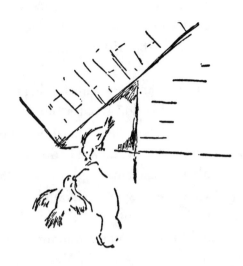

For a moment or two he fluttered there, but he couldn't get into the small opening with his cargo. So he flew back down again and left the paper on the ground behind him. Then he returned to the eaves again and disappeared inside for a second. Soon, not only he came out, but his wife also, and they both cocked their heads and peered down at the piece of tissue paper. They were obviously formulating a plan.

With his wife watching intently, the sparrow flew back down to the grass. Again he managed to pick up the paper and again he flew back to the threshold of his house with it. He fluttered about, keeping his balance, just outside the opening to the eaves. As he fluttered close by, his wife reached out her bill and took the tissue paper from him, backing into the opening with it, the triumphant husband following her in.

This was just about the smartest thing that Rachel had ever seen a bird do. What a fine sheet for the sparrows' nest the tissue paper must have made, she thought drowsily. When Rachel had written to Papa telling him about these smart sparrows, he had written back saying she was so observant he would have to make her his assistant.

What could ever be more wonderful than that? Rachel asked herself. "Call in Mr. Pye," the men in Washington would say, and, "Bring Rachel Pye too," they would surely add.

Rachel was getting very sleepy. After all she had been up since dawn with bee-bite. Through half-closed eyes she watched the perpendicular swimmer swimming downwards and swimming upwards; and she watched her brother Jerry swimming back and forth across the reservoir; and affectionately she watched the little puppy snoozing; and drowsily she watched the water flies skimming over the surface of the pond, darting zigzaggedly this way and that, bumping into one another like hockey players on ice; and she listened to Duke's happy hunting in the woods behind her. And when Duke came back to the rock to rest himself and to keep an eye on his master, whose perpendicular swimming he had no use for, she lazily scratched his back and he sleepily scratched his stomach. And as she, lanky Duke, and little Ginger were drowsing on the sunny rock, she heard a rustling in the woods behind her.

"Just a chipmunk," Rachel assured herself. "Or a squirrel."

But Ginger waked up and he bristled the short hair on his back; and lazy Duke raised his big jowly head, looking puzzled. *It couldn't be a chipmunk or Duke would go after it,* thought Rachel. *And it couldn't be the man in blue because he is still way way away on his rock. Could it be Unsavory?* she asked herself. *Of course not,* she answered herself.

Since she heard no more she tried not to think of Unsavory because it was an uncomfortable thing to do—to think about Unsavory while she was alone on the big rock, guarding Ginger pup. Jerry was on the other side of the reservoir now, and Dick Badger was so occupied with his up-and-down swimming he would not have heard her if she called him. In the quiet she heard another rustling. Trying to sound carefree, but to be on the safe side, she called Jerry.

"Jer-ry!" she yelled.

A small breeze was stirring and maybe the rustling she had heard was breezes only, but she felt lonely. Just then a hat fell into the water exactly where Dick Badger was swimming and as he came up for air, he came up right under this hat. He threw it off and sputtered and laughed and said, "Where'd this old hat come from?"

Rachel said, "I don't know. It just flew into the water." In the dazzling sunshine she had not seen yet that this hat was yellow! Dick Badger swam up to the rock with the hat. He was going to play games with it, throw it into the water and swim to it, have him and Jerry race to it. But Jerry came back just then, and he and Rachel eyed the hat speechlessly. It was a muddy mustard-yellowish hat! They dropped the hat on the rock as though it was poison and they looked toward the woods not knowing what to expect next.

"I heard a rustling," whispered Rachel. She was so scared tears popped into her eyes. "That's why I called."

But now they heard nothing and they saw no one. They thought the person might be up in a big tree but the branches and leaves were too thick to see anything.

"Hey!" shouted Jerry.

Only silence answered him.

"If you want your old hat, come and get it," yelled Jerry bravely, hoping the person would stay where he was nevertheless. But still there was only silence. It was eerie.

"Sick 'em up, Duke," said Dick, delighted to be part of the mystery.

When you said, "Sick 'em up" to Duke, or "Rats!" he would usually just raise his mournful face and sniff a few times, looking sad. Or else, to please you, he would lumber off a few paces as though he had a purpose in mind. No one who knew Duke was the slightest bit scared of him. However, he was such a big hound that if Dick sicked him on a person who didn't know him, that person would be scared out of his wits.

Now Ginger, on the other hand, when you said, "Sick 'em up" to him, bristled his back, got into a rage, and tore around like mad. And this he would have done now, only Rachel kept a tight hold of him and all he could do was growl, the way he did with his orange duster.

Duke hadn't budged. He had only raised his head and stared with a wise expression into the woods. "Sick 'em up," said Dick again. Duke lumbered agreeably off into the woods but he soon came back and lay down lazily again, licking his paws noisily.

Jerry and Dick flung off their wet trunks and got into their clothes. They all decided to go home. They weren't going off into the woods looking for the mysterious footstepper, that was certain. But there, on the rock, lay the hat, wet and battered and muddy yellow, and what would they do with it? Leave it here? Or pitch it into the reservoir way way out? It would serve the mean man right to lose his hat. Or perhaps they should take it home with them and keep it as "Exhibit A." No. Then the person would come prowling around looking for his old hat and what they wanted was for him to go away and leave them alone.

Finally they left the hat on the rock. "Hey, I know what," said Dick Badger. "I have a piece of red crayon in my pocket. We'll put a little mark in the hat and if we see anyone in this hat again we'll know it's the same person who has been snooping on us up here at the res'. We'll know that much at least."

This Dick Badger did. He put a small red mark inside the leather band of the old felt hat and they left the hat there on the rock, to be picked up by whomever it belonged to.

"I think it must have been Unsavory," said Rachel. "Or else the person would have said, 'Hey. That's my hat. Please throw it back.'"

This sounded logical. "Unless," said Jerry, who wanted to exhaust all possibilities, "it happened to be just any old hat lying around up here, belonging to no one; and it just happened to blow into the reservoy."

"Um-m-m," said Rachel. "It might have blown off a scarecrow in some farmer's garden, up Barney Hill a ways."

"Um-m-m," said Dick skeptically, for he preferred it to be part of the mystery. "Except that all
the scarecrows I ever knew had black hats on 'em,
not yellow."

"Nope," said Rachel and Jerry, agreeing.

Anyway, they left the old hat with its red mark
in it that wouldn't wash off because it was indelible.
And they went back across the little dam and past
the red mill where, in the deep woods, gloaming
had set in, and then out into the wooded path, still
half in the gloaming and half in the sunlight, past
Speedys' barn and the last houses, and then, there
they were at the Green again.

As they walked, for Dick Badger's benefit, for
he never tired of the mystery, they reviewed the
times they had been watched or followed. There was
the person standing in the doorway of the church
when Rachel was in the pulpit, but that may have
been the minister, so he really could not be counted.
There was the person racing and crouching over the
telephone poles in back of Speedys' barn the day
they went to buy Ginger. There were the mysterious
footsteps that night coming home from Gramma's,
and the glimpse, under the horse chestnut tree, of
a yellowish hat.

There was, also, the hat at the fence yesterday,
spied first by Uncle Bennie in his high chair. Now,

there was the rustle in the woods. And there was the hat itself falling right in the water where the perpendicular swimmer was coming up for air. Was all this the same hat and person, or what? It wasn't imaginary anymore, that was certain, all this mystery, all this carrying on. For here was a real, honest-to-goodness, ugly, yellow, felt hat, that they had left on the rock with a red mark in it.

When they reached home they told Mama the episode of the hat and she said, "Well . . ." And then she said, "Your father is coming home tonight and we'll ask him what he thinks."

That night, when Mr. Pye got home, he was told everything, all about the getting of Ginger Pye, and the mysterious footstepper—everything. But he didn't think anything. He just said, "Um-m-m." He was busy thinking about birds, especially the birds on Mount Pisgah from which he had just returned, and that was why he didn't think anything about all this hat, footsteps, and rustling business. And since Mr. Pye just said, "Um-m-m," none of the story sounded important anymore. What was wonderful was that Papa was home now. He was going to stay home for a long long time, he said.

6

Ginger on the Fire Escape

The unsavory character may have been the real enemy in Ginger Pye's life but of this Ginger was unaware. He was a very happy dog and the only enemy he knew he had was an enemy dog.

It was October now and no more had been heard or seen of Unsavory, his hat, or his footsteps. In fact, such a long time had passed since the affair of the hat at the reservoir that everyone had begun to forget about the unsavory character.

"He knows, everybody knows, that Ginger is my puppy now, and I guess he has given up," said Jerry to Rachel.

"Um-m-m," agreed Rachel.

It was during these weeks that Ginger discovered the enemy dog. It was lucky that Ginger did find out about him for whom else could he play with? School had started but what did Ginger understand of school? All he understood was that, for some reason, Jerry and Rachel now abandoned him for a great deal of each day. Therefore, in whom could Ginger take an interest if not in the enemy dog and for a while he was obsessed with the very idea of him.

The enemy dog lived in the tall pier glass mirror, at least that was where Ginger first saw him—the tall pier glass mirror that stood between two windows

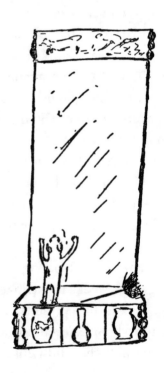

in the horsehair parlor. This mirror had been a wedding present to the Pyes; and the three large vases that stood in its marble base were also wedding presents. One day Ginger was reaching up for his orange duster that happened to be lying on the marble base, and it was then that he made his amazing discovery.

There was another dog in this house and he was in the shiny mirror! Yet, all along, Ginger had mistakenly thought he was the only dog in this house.

Ginger Pye gave this new dog a friendly woof for he did not realize all in a second that this was his enemy dog that was going to torment him and stay in shiny places. The dog gave Ginger a friendly woof too, only Ginger couldn't hear it. Ginger Pye then barked loudly at the new dog and the new dog barked back at Ginger, only still he made no sound. His woofing and his barking were silent and, because of this, rather exasperating.

Ginger made a dash for the dog in the mirror and the dog in the mirror made a dash for Ginger. They growled at each other, Ginger in his loud fashion and the new dog in his silent fashion. Their noses were plastered right close together, so close Ginger couldn't even see the other dog anymore. But the cowardly dog stayed inside where he was good and safe and he wouldn't come out. It was infuriating and it made Ginger Pye frantic.

It was then that Ginger realized that this dog in the mirror was an enemy dog and not a friendly companion.

Moreover, it turned out that the dog did not stay inside his pier glass mirror after all. He cropped up in other places, in other mirrors, in the window-panes, even in Ginger's own eating pan, eating up Ginger's dinner. And outside the house, he might be met up with too. For he was also a water dog, staying in puddles, the reservoir, the harbor, and the Sound.

Once Jerry and Rachel took Ginger for a walk over to Gramma's. They went by way of the shore instead of the street and it was a most interesting excursion. The tide was low. Periwinkles and horse-shoe crabs lay on the beaches, and clams were spouting here and there in the wet mud of low tide. The children crawled under every little red boat-house, smelling the wonderful stale sea smells there. They walked out on every wobbly little wooden pier. And everywhere Ginger delightedly frisked ahead of them.

It went to Ginger's head to be with Jerry and Rachel on such an unusual expedition. He picked up dry chunks of wood for them to throw and he tried to nudge the horseshoe crabs into getting a move on. He had no thought of the enemy dog. He was a carefree happy dog and he was always the first one out to the end of the little piers. There he barked at the water endlessly stretching, at the sky, the singing gulls, the bobbing buoys.

At the end of one weather-beaten shaky old pier, to which a little boat was tied and placidly rocking, Ginger happened, for the first time, to look straight down into the queer green water. And there, looking up at him, was his enemy, the dog!

Now Ginger was the dog of Jerry Pye. The enemy dog was not. Yet here he was, right here in the green-blue sea. Apparently he had tagged along, sneakily, all the way, hoping to become the dog of Jerry Pye. These were Ginger's thoughts as he dived into the water, with Jerry and Rachel shouting earnest instructions to him from above. Ginger had never before been in such deep water and could he swim, they wanted to know.

"Ginger, can you swim?" yelled Rachel.

"Of course he can," said Jerry. "Look at him. Swims like he's swum all his life."

It was true. Ginger could swim and he managed to get back to dry land in a very accomplished and intense fashion. He felt refreshed from his brisk saltwater swim and he rolled over and over in the warm sand happily.

"He's always thinking himself in mirrors and water is his enemy." Rachel laughed.

"Um-m-m," agreed Jerry. "I'd hate to meet the real enemy, old Unsavory, along here in one of these old boathouses."

"O-o-o-h," gasped Rachel, stunned at such a prospect.

But they didn't. And neither did Ginger happen

to have any further encounters with the enemy dog on that trip. He enjoyed a pleasant relaxed afternoon with Uncle Bennie and Jerry and Rachel, and he chased Gramma's chickens, getting a pecking or two, and he tasted Gramma's homemade peach ice cream, spitting out the hard cold lumps of peach as Rachel and Jerry were doing, likewise. He really never expected to see the enemy dog again, having jumped on him in the water that way, scaring him out of his wits.

But of course, he did. When he got home the enemy dog was right there again, in the tall pier glass mirror, tongue hanging out thirstily, ears drooping tiredly. Secretly Ginger was glad to have the other dog back so he would have him handy for future bouts when life at home, without Jerry and Rachel, became too tame.

Soon after this wonderful expedition along the shore, however, Ginger began to suspect that the enemy dog was himself. He gave up pursuit of him in preference to the pursuit of cats. Cats certainly did not stay inside shiny things and they really came out to fight. They were a more satisfactory type of enemy than the enemy dog had been.

During the time when everyone had been worried about the unsavory character Ginger had been kept in the backyard unless he was with some person. Now, however, he was allowed in either the front or the backyard. It was impossible to keep Ginger from slipping out of the house with Gracie-the-cat anyway, for Gracie had the knack of opening the front door by leaping up and undoing the latch.

So Ginger now had the run of the land. Naturally, he preferred the front to the back of the house. From the front he could survey the entire neighborhood, get into other yards besides his own, and chase all the cats.

There was a matter that had begun to bother Ginger, however, and it had nothing to do with cats or the enemy dog. It was this. Where did Jerry disappear every morning and afternoon with his tiresome, "Go home, Ginger!" And Rachel, too. Where did they go?

Ginger's feelings were hurt, being deserted this way, even though Jerry patted him and gave him fond scratches behind the ear and such attentions before tearing out the front door saying, "I'm late again, by jiminy."

"Where could he go, anyway?" puzzled Ginger. Today he intended to find out. Ginger was a purposeful dog. Once he had decided to do something, he did it, provided he was not obstructed by some person. Now was the time, he felt, to investigate the constant goings away and comings back of his master, Jerry Pye, and of the master's sister, Rachel Pye. They had something to do with the goings past the house and the returnings past the house, twice a day, of all the boys and girls in Cranbury, practically. Wherever they all went, it might possibly be more fun than chasing cats, more fun, even, than going up to the reservoir.

At this moment Ginger happened to be lying opposite the tall pier glass mirror surveying himself with a thoughtful planning look. He arose, stretched, and gave himself a challenging yap for old times' sake. He made a dash for Gracie-the-cat, leaped over her imploring crouching form, and went into the kitchen. After a few laps of water he looked around for something of Jerry's to smell, to get the scent well fixed in his scent department.

He found Jerry's sweater slung over the back of a kitchen chair and he pulled it to the floor and thrust his nose in its folds. Thoughtfully and earnestly he breathed in the essence of Jerry until it permeated his entire being, down to his toes and the tip of his short tail. His heart thumped with delight and he thought excitedly, now, now, he was going to find Jerry. "Jerry, Jerry, Jerry," his heart sang.

Of course Ginger knew the Jerry smell perfectly

without having to rely on Jerry's old sweater. But this was to be his first experience at real hard trailing. It could not be compared with the easy following of the fresh trail of a dog, a cat, a chicken, or a chipmunk. Jerry had left some time ago. This meant a real hard trailing job and Ginger did not want to fail.

The first rule in trailing was, get the smell thoroughly inside himself. The next was, nose to ground. He had the smell. So now, nose to ground. He pushed his nose along the floor to the front door and paused, for the moment, stalled.

Fortunately, just then Gracie-the-cat decided to go outdoors herself. She leaped in the air in her own smart fashion, sprung open the latch, and she and Ginger Pye went outside, leaving the door open behind them. And there Ginger Pye was, on his front lawn, surveying the scene.

At this moment, who should be coming home from the grocery store, her arms filled with bags and bundles, her face stern, as stern as her gentle face could get, but Mrs. Pye.

"Ginger," said Mrs. Pye. "Where are you going? You are not to chase Mrs. Carruthers' cat anymore. And there has been a complaint that you chased a chicken. Mrs. Finney told me in the grocery store.

If you keep up this outrageous behavior, you shall have to stay on the leash!"

Leash! Hated hateful word. Ginger shuddered. The leash was coiled like a snake on the stoop right now. It was an awful thing to have on the neck. Ginger had suspected it was awful and he was wary of it the first time Jerry fastened it on. But he had not imagined, no dog could possibly imagine, how very awful, how completely horrible a leash was, until he had one on.

When he had the leash on Ginger would struggle and struggle to get it off, pawing at it, shaking his head wildly, and showing the whites of his eyes. And if, forgetting for a moment he had the dreadful thing on, he made a dash for the Carruthers' cat, wham! The leash would nearly break his neck and down he would fall, gasping and rolling on the sidewalk. Jerry's concern over him would be pleasant, that was all that was pleasant about the leash.

"Aw, Ginger," Jerry would say. "You mustn't tug at the leash so."

Whenever Ginger saw the leash coming he would cower and quiver, hoping Jerry would change his mind and put it, perhaps, on Gracie instead.

But Jerry would say, "Now come on, Ginger. You've got to learn to walk nice on the leash."

Ginger merely strained the harder, and struggled and tugged and chortled and gasped and dragged Jerry along.

"Walk nice, Ginger," pleaded Jerry. And he would point out other dogs that pranced along neatly at the end of their leashes with never a gasp or a choke. The owners of these dogs would walk along in dignity or jauntiness, in an upright position and not in this disgraceful jerking struggling fashion.

"That way, not this way," urged Jerry.

"You must train him," suggested Mama.

"I'm tryin'," said Jerry gloomily. "But he won't walk nice."

Jerry did try to train Ginger. Once he even spanked him. Nothing did any good, not even bribery with candy. Ginger continued to gasp and choke and drag. Sneeze, he would do for Jerry. Shake hands, he would do for Jerry. Beg, walk on his hind feet, and be dead dog. But walk nice on the leash? Never.

At last Jerry gave up trying to train him to walk nice on the leash. He would carry the leash along with him on their excursions, and he would put it on after Ginger had chased a cat or a chicken. *After*, not before.

Soliloquizing in this manner with his nose in the grass, Ginger looked meekly up at Mrs. Pye who still towered over him with her bags and potatoes and things. He was winning, he thought. Mrs. Pye no longer looked so stern; her eyes were laughing in fact. But to assure victory, Ginger cringed. He was not cringing in his heart. But if he presented a humble front, he thought Mrs. Pye would not bother him anymore and he could finish that which he had started to do. And what was that? Chase Mrs. Carruthers' cat? Goodness no. He had almost forgotten. Interruptions were so bad for the game of scent trailing. But he remembered now. He was on the trail of Jerry Pye, his master.

Concealing his impatience, since the leash was still handy, Ginger looked up at Mrs. Pye with what, in the past, he had found to be a winning pose, head to side, tongue dangling out. Mrs. Pye gave him a little pat, spilling out all her potatoes as she did so. Of course Ginger had to help gather these up, by making a game of it, nosing them all over the lawn. When finally all the potatoes were recaptured Mrs. Pye said, "There, there. I didn't mean to be cross, Ginger. But you must be a good dog, do you hear?"

And at last she went into the house leaving Ginger on the front lawn with his nose buried in a patch of thick short grass that was just covered with Jerry scent. Jerry must have flipped his knife here, dropped his books here, or something. Ginger decided he'd better be on the trail before Mrs. Pye again thought of putting the hated leash on him, or of giving him a bath, or a brushing. So. Now. Nose to ground.

Leaving his own yard and going on past Dick Badger's, it was easy enough to follow the Jerry scent, and Ginger pasted his nose to that scent. It led past the Carruthers' house. Actually without sniffing so hard, Ginger knew this was the direction Jerry had taken because he could always see him this far. However, in trailing, a dog has to sniff and snort like the dickens because that is the way it is done. He kept his nose plastered to the ground and he was concentrating so hard his whole face was pushed in and wrinkled up. It looked as though he were pushing his nose up the street in front of him. He kept getting sand up his nose and he had to wheeze it out of himself in long deep exhalings. This was hard work, but it was wonderful work, and it was apparent he was born to be a regular trail hound even though he was mostly fox terrier.

Now Ginger was going past the Carruthers' driveway. He paused for a moment with his nose glued to the pavement. He was still drawing in the Jerry scent, but it had merely crossed his mind to wonder whether or not the long-haired orange Carruthers' cat was anywhere around.

Keeping his nose plastered to the ground, not moving his head one inch, he turned his eyes way to the corners so that from in front one could have seen only the whites. Then, from out of the corners of his eyes, he spied her, spied the Carruthers' cat sitting under a rosebush, her favorite spot, watching for birds. Her back was to him. She was, perhaps, not aware that brave Ginger was right here?

He could surprise her. He could corner her, that was what he certainly could do, before she had a chance to run up a tree. His eyes turned back to his nose. He snuffed in the Jerry smell. Jerry, Jerry, where are you anyway? His eyes roved back to the cat. She had caught sight of him and all her fur was electric and stiff. But she had not run. She was in exactly the mood in which he loved to engage her in battle.

Still, Ginger did not give chase. Again he sniffed deeply of the Jerry scent. Then, a little sadly, he started shoving his nose up the street again. He had won over temptation. He snuffed on for a few paces when, "Pfsht!" The Gaines' cat, a tremendous gray one, spit insultingly in his direction and turned and fled challengingly into the Gaines' vast backyard.

Ginger couldn't help it. He forgot his quest. After the Gaines' cat he dashed, sneezing the gravel out of his nose as he went. He ran so fast he skidded around the corner to the backyard. From there, presently, his short sharp yelps and the cat's long venomous hisses and yowls echoed in the quiet of a school morning in Cranbury.

Fifteen minutes later Ginger ran jauntily out from the Gaines' backyard where the old gray cat was now up a huge red mulberry tree. One of Ginger's ears was torn and bleeding, true. And he had clawings on the white fur of his back. But he didn't care, for it had been a glorious bout.

Happy though Ginger felt, all tingling and exhilarated, nevertheless there was something bothering him deep inside himself that kept him from feeling the complete contentment a fight with a cat usually inspired in him. He could not immediately put his paw on this certain something. It was like a bone he knew he had somewhere that he couldn't recall the exact location of.

He lay panting on the soft green grass in his own front yard again. Mrs. Pye came out and said, "Oh, there you are, Ginger. Good dog," and she went back in again.

Ginger wagged his tail self-righteously. He licked his paw and applied it to his wounded ear. He should improve his technique with the Gaines' cat for he had received too many digs. Ginger felt vaguely dissatisfied with himself, and melancholy. He knew his hurting ear, alone, was not the cause of this feeling, for Jerry could fix that. Jerry would put something cool and soothing on it. Jerry . . . Jerry . . . Oh, Jerry! That was what it was! There Ginger had been—on the trail of Jerry, to find out where he went always. And then this! This fight with a cat! He had fallen into temptation after all. What a reflection upon his character!

In his shame Ginger stuck his tail down tight. He felt like a traitor, a deserter. But there was still time. He could still go and find Jerry. He had started out to do one thing and he had ended by doing another. All right. It would not happen again because he was Ginger, the purposeful dog. His tail perked up and he pasted his nose to the ground again.

This time, as Ginger steered his nose past the Carruthers' and the Gaines' tempting houses, all he permitted himself was a slight reminiscent wag of the tail. That was all. Not even a peek from the corners of his eyes. And from his mind he banished thoughts of all the eyes of all the hidden cats that probably were on him. Scrunching up his nose, pushing it on up the street, he lost himself completely in following the trail of Jerry Pye.

At a certain point, going through a small field, the scent led Ginger to a little crabapple tree. He stood on his hind legs and inhaled the scent as far up the tree as he could thrust his nose. Jerry had been up this tree but he certainly was no longer there for, of course, there would be a much keener scent if he were. The quest was by no means over.

Ginger remained poised there against the tree in contemplation. Jerry's going up the tree might be what was known as a decoy. Decoys were difficult, though not impossible, to outwit. For instance, the person a dog was trailing might leap from treetop to treetop. A dog had to work doubly hard and might have to explore in every direction before finding the trail again. But then, that is all part of tracking.

Ginger wagged his tail in appreciation of his master's cleverness and he keenly anticipated matching his wits against his. No doubt, Jerry had suspected that Ginger would try to trail him. So, up the tree he had gone to throw Ginger off his tracks.

Thus Ginger analyzed the difficult situation before leaping down. He then began spiritedly to go round and round the tree in ever-widening circles. By the time he was ten dog-lengths away from the tree his nose picked up the scent again. And the decoy was over.

Apparently Jerry had swung out of the tree on a limber branch and had landed way over here on all fours. Here, also, was one of Jerry's pencils with Ginger's tooth marks on it as well as Jerry's own. Jerry had then proceeded in the same direction as before the tree decoy, and this Ginger did likewise, with the pencil in his mouth.

The pencil made trailing considerably more difficult than hitherto, if not well-nigh impossible. In the end, Ginger had to drop the pencil, find the trail, go back for the pencil, and bring it to the farthest point of trailing. Of course he could not abandon the pencil. The going, therefore, was slower now, not only because of the complication of the pencil, but also because suddenly there seemed to be a very great many more smells to weed out before locating Jerry's.

Ginger snorted and blew and carefully cherished the faint but certain scent that was Jerry's. So close to the ground did he keep his nose, he bumped right into the cement stoop of a candy store. He raised his head, sniffing expertly and gently. He allowed the enticing chocolate and peanut smells to mingle with Jerry's.

Was it possible that here was the end of the trail, the end of the long quest? Did Jerry spend all those hours away from him in a candy store? How marvelous, if true. He wagged his tail expectantly. His mouth drooled, for he loved candy, and he trotted into the candy store.

Jerry was not there, Ginger soon found out as he sniffed busily around the floor, eating bits of sweet that had been dropped and giving an excited bark when he found a piece of sticky paper Jerry had thrown down. It had had licorice in it—not one of Ginger's favorites; one of Jerry's though.

Ginger chewed all the sweetness out of the paper

and reluctantly let that go. After all, he had still to push his nose and Jerry's pencil up the street and that was just about all he could manage. The trail was certainly hot now, what with having found Jerry's pencil and then this piece of sticky paper. Yes, this was what was known as being "hot on the trail."

Sniff, sniff here. Snort and blow there. A great, great many feet had passed this way and Ginger lost the trail. He just followed the lead of all those feet and at last he paused to take his bearings. He looked about him. He had come through the wide open gate of a tall brown wooden fence and here he was, in an enormous yard, half pavement and half worn-down grass. He lay down on a little patch of this grass close to a big brick building. His nose stung and his neck ached from the long push and hard concentration. The pencil lay safely between his paws. He licked his tongue over his dry nose until it became moist and cool again, and he studied the building before him.

The building was big, hard, and brick. If this was where Jerry came every day and spent his time, Ginger was no longer envious. Why come here, though? Why come here when he and Jerry could tramp up Shingle Hill or tear through the woods around the reservoir picking up acorns and finding frogs? Still, inside might be pleasanter than outside, and Ginger toured the building to find a way in.

All doors were closed. All Ginger could do now was to sit and wait for Jerry to come out. Imagine Jerry's pleasure when he saw his faithful dog waiting here for him, choosing to wait here for him instead of chasing cats, moreover.

Ginger lazily crossed his front paws the way he always did while resting. He felt drowsy. Now and then he twitched his back to get rid of a fly circling around in the warm October sunshine. He listened to the sounds coming from the big building. There was a sound as of many bees droning. A sharp voice gave a command and this droning stopped. The sharp voice gave another command and there was a burst of singing. "Hats off, hats off, the flag is passing by." This was pleasant and Ginger was sorry when it stopped. After the singing there was quiet for a time, with only an occasional sharp command from the one in charge of all these goings-on.

The long quest, the warm sunshine, the quiet, all contributed to Ginger's sleepiness. With one vigilant eye half open, he began to nod.

Then—was he dreaming? He heard Jerry's voice. Jerry's voice loud and clear and all by itself. Ginger sat up. His tail began uncertainly to wag. Then it wagged uncontrollably, for he was not dreaming. Jerry's voice was coming loud and clear from one of the high windows. Jerry was not using his regular voice that he used with Ginger or with any of the Pyes. He was using a high and loud and clear voice. But it was Jerry's voice, even so.

Ginger listened, in a transport of delight. Then he gave a short bark announcing, if Jerry cared to know, that he, Ginger, was right out here. Not only was he out here, he would manage to get to Jerry somehow, so there would be no more separation.

Ginger no longer felt tired. He tore around the building barking and wagging not only his tail, wagging his whole body. He was looking again for a way in. All entrances were closed. He came back and longingly stared up at the window from which he judged Jerry's voice was coming. Jerry was still talking, though the one in command kept butting in.

There was a perilous-looking iron stairway leading up to the open window through which Jerry's voice was floating. Standing beneath this curious stairway Ginger could see sky through the open work of the steps. Cautiously Ginger put one paw on the bottom step. It was hard to get a grip on but at least it did not wobble. He put his other front paw on the bottom step and carefully pulled his body up onto it.

The main difficulty was that his paws kept sliding through the iron bars. What peculiar stairs. No carpets at all, as at home. Even so, by being extremely cautious, he might be able to drag himself to the next story, pencil and all.

Carefully, step by step, Ginger crawled up the extraordinary stairs. This was not a decoy. This was a dangerous undertaking. He did not dare look down between those iron bars. He had looked down once and nearly dropped Jerry's pencil out of terror. Up, up, up he crept until there at last he was—at the open window. Gasping in relief Ginger climbed onto the windowsill and stood there, drooling, pencil in mouth, tail wagging in delighted expectation.

This room happened to be filled with boys and girls all seated at little desks. They looked sleepy and the place did not seem anywhere near as enticing as up at the reservoir. But anyway, there was Jerry, standing by his seat, his voice coming out clear and high and loud again.

The teacher issued a command. "Read it again, Jerry, more distinctly, and pay more attention to your final g's."

"My dog, Ginger," read Jerry Pye, and he cleared his throat.

Well. When Ginger heard Jerry say his name

he let out one short yelp of greeting. Ginger! "Yes, here I am, right here, Jerry," was what his bark meant. Of course he dropped Jerry's pencil but fortunately it dropped on the windowsill and not down below. Ginger quickly picked it up again and held it triumphantly in his mouth.

The minute Ginger let out that little yelp of greeting, what a hullabaloo came over the place. Some little girls screamed and some laughed. All

the boys cheered. The person in command clapped her hands but no one paid any attention to her. Jerry dropped the paper he was holding and for a moment he stared at Ginger, too stunned for words or action. Then he rushed to the window and patted his dog to make him feel at home.

Ginger jumped into the room, dropped Jerry's pencil at his feet and looked up at Jerry. He was inviting him to throw it so he could run after it and bring it back, the way they played the rock game at home, or ball, or stick.

Jerry picked up his pencil. "He even found my pencil I lost on the way to school this morning," he said in greater astonishment than ever. "What a smart dog!"

"Your dog?" asked Oliver Peacock, a boy with glasses, in admiration.

"Yeh," said Jerry proudly. "My dog. Trailed me here."

"The dog brought a pencil with him because it's school," shrilled one little girl.

"Whew!" whistled Oliver Peacock.

Ginger wagged his tail and looked as though he were laughing, the way he always did when he understood that pleasant things were being spoken of him. He licked Jerry's hand. So. Here he was! It was not much of a place but if Jerry could put up with it, so could he. He trotted around the room, his toenails making a pitter-patter. He smelled here and sniffed there. In one corner by a cupboard he kept his nose glued for some time. There was the possibility of mice there.

He detoured around the tall person who was still clapping and giving orders that no one was minding any more than he minded anyone when he was off after a cat.

Suddenly the tall one took a long stick and she brought this down on her desk with such a bang it broke in two and went sailing through the air.

"Quiet!" she bellowed.

The hullabaloo stopped short then. This was a welcome relief to Ginger who did not see how Jerry stood this sort of a noisy life. His ears hurt him.

"Jared Pye!" the tall one said. "Either take your dog home or make him lie down under your desk until dismissal time which is, thank merciful heavens, only a few minutes away. And, Jared," she added. "See that this disgraceful performance is not repeated or I shall have to report you to Mr. Pennypepper. Even so, you shall stand in the corner all this afternoon," she promised.

"Always the same old punishments," groaned Dick Badger wearily to Jerry.

"Come here, Ginger," said Jerry. As though he

could help it, he thought, if the dog he owned happened to be so smart he could trail him all the way to school. You would think the teacher could see that, wouldn't you? he asked himself. "Come here, pup," he urged.

Ginger recognized the pleading note in Jerry's voice and he pattered over to him, for he wanted nothing to do with the tall one and her sticks and shrill voice.

"Lie down, Ginger," said Jerry. "Dead dog," he begged.

Being awfully tired, Ginger was happy to lie down. He licked his nose with loud smacking noises and he washed his torn and bleeding ear, and he washed himself all over. He was right under Jerry's desk and every now and then Jerry gave him a nice pat with his foot.

There was complete silence now except for Ginger's loud paw licking and the occasional loud nose blowing of the tall one. In this quiet Ginger stopped licking himself. With a contented sigh he slipped into a thoughtful doze. He scarcely did more than twitch his ears when, from another room, he heard some more of the droning, as of bees, that he had heard outside. Now he could hear what the droning was saying, though.

R-A-T rat. C-A-T cat. Apparently the boys and girls were being instructed in the best way to manage these creatures. As for Ginger, he was too tired to listen and, besides, he knew the best way to handle them. As though one had to come to a place like this to learn such things.

There was one big boy, and his name was Wally Bullwinkle, and he did not take his eyes off Ginger Pye for one minute. He pretended to be lost in his big geography book, but he had a hand over his face and from between his fingers he was studying Ginger with a sly and furtive mien. Nobody—not Ginger, not Jerry—nobody noticed this.

7

The Disappearance of Ginger Pye on Thanksgiving Day

Ginger was a quite famous dog now, in Cranbury, for his achievement on the school fire escape and for other happy ventures. Almost everyone knew him and liked him. He had a great many friends that he liked to call on. When visiting, he never cut across people's lawns, unless, of course, distracted by a cat. He always walked up the sidewalk or up the driveway, the polite way that people do. He had a comical sidewise gait and it was an amusing sight to see him purposefully walking up the street and turning into somebody's walk and trotting up on the porch and scratching at the door to be let in for a visit and a pat and perhaps a bone.

"Here comes Ginger Pye," people would say, delighted to be honored with a visit from such a famous dog.

It was impossible to think of Ginger having one single enemy in the wide world and the Pyes had long ago tucked all thought of the unsavory character in the backs of their minds. For there had been no more suspicious happenings since the first few days of Ginger's coming into the family. The Pyes were all proud of their famous dog, though of course they did not boast of him.

Now Ginger was going to be even more famous than ever before though not, this time, in a happy way. For a dreadful thing happened.

Ginger disappeared!

The terrible discovery was made at four o'clock in the afternoon on Thanksgiving Day, right after the Pyes had finished dinner. Mr. Pye had returned the night before from another trip, this time to the Sea Islands, studying more birds. Gramma and Grampa and Uncle Bennie were also here and dinner had lasted a very long time. This was natural since it was Thanksgiving Day and there were three roast chickens and plenty of drumsticks.

Ginger had grown tired of all the talking and the eating and he had scratched at the front door to be let out. "Don't let the puppy out in front," said Mrs. Pye. "Mrs. Carruthers and Mrs. Gaines are sick and tired of all the barking at and chasing of their cats. Let us have some peace and quiet on Thanksgiving Day."

So Jerry let Ginger out the back door into their

own enclosed backyard. They heard Ginger crying piteously for a time, because he had wanted to seek adventure on the street. Instead, there he was in the backyard with no possibility of getting out, at least so everyone thought.

The backyard had high board fences on three sides of it, and on the fourth side, the front side, wire fencing joined up with the board fences. Currant bushes grew along the wire fence and they were spiky and cold-looking in the November air. The wire fence and the board fences were all in good condition. There were no loose boards or holes, and Ginger could not get out. Yet Ginger had gotten out, and how? That was what everybody wanted to know.

Jerry was the one who made the discovery. When dinner at last was over, he had gone out to play with his lonesome dog. But there was no dog, lonesome or otherwise. He was gone. It would be impossible to explain why Jerry had such a terrible sinking feeling in the pit of his stomach. It seemed to him that the emptiness in the backyard was a long-time emptiness, that Ginger had been gone a long long while.

Someone must have let Ginger back into the house without my knowing it, he thought.

But no one had. Still, perhaps he had got in somehow, on someone's heels without being noticed, perhaps when Mama went out for the celery. Once he was in, perhaps Gracie-the-cat had unlatched the front door for him in her unusual-for-a-cat manner. But Gracie-the-cat was innocently and languorously sprawled on the mantel. The latch was tightly fastened on the front door. No one had let Ginger in or out of any door except Jerry when he let him out the back one into the backyard. And the backyard was where he still should be, safe and sound.

It was unbelievable that Ginger was not out there somewhere and Jerry went to the back door and whistled. Nothing but that empty silence answered. Jerry then toured the house, the bedrooms, the parlor, even Papa's study in the tower, but Ginger most certainly was not at home.

Rachel was helping Mama and Gramma with the dishes and there were mountains of these. It looked as though dishwashing would last a week. Uncle Bennie was curled up asleep on the couch in the living room, having had too much to eat. "Take a little nap. Take a little nap," Gramma had urged him. And this time Uncle Bennie had not refused. Grampa and Papa were in the little parlor sitting on the scratchy horsehair furniture, talking in low tones in order not to wake up Uncle Bennie. No one was as excited as Jerry about the disappearance of Ginger except Rachel.

"Oh, he probably got out of the yard somehow and is off chasing cats," Mama said reassuringly.

It might be true, Jerry thought. Nobody in Cranbury had such a smart puppy as he had—a puppy that could trail a boy through the streets and climb up the fire escape at school and find Jerry in his own room, Room Nine, at school, and bring his pencil to him that he had lost somewhere along the way. It would not be too surprising for a dog such as that to find a way to get out of the backyard. Perhaps he had dug a hole under the fence and perhaps he was somewhere in the neighborhood. Later Jerry would examine all the fences and stop up whatever hole he might have dug.

So Jerry went out the front door and down the street a ways and he whistled for Ginger, seven short whistles with an uptilt on the last whistle, the way he always did, and then he listened. No little brown-and-white dog came tearing like dynamite. Nowhere in the neighborhood was there the sound of Ginger's special cat and chicken barking. The silence of Thanksgiving Day, with everyone sitting around with stomachs full and eyes heavy, was all the answer there was to Jerry's whistling.

Except for that time when Ginger had trailed Jerry to school, so far as anyone knew, Ginger had never left their block before. His going away like this was puzzling and it was frightening. Jerry ran next door to ask Dick Badger if he had seen his dog, but no one answered the bell and then he remembered that Dick's family was spending the day with the Badger clan in Cheshire. Disconsolately Jerry returned home where everyone was still doing the same things.

Rachel looked at Jerry and she was as anxious and panic-stricken as he was. After all, it had been he and she together who had heard the mysterious footsteps that first night long ago, had seen the yellow hat of the unsavory character in the lamplight and up at the reservoir; and she loved Ginger as much as Jerry did; and Ginger was as much her dog as he was Jerry's with the exception that he had been Jerry's idea in the first place, not hers.

She dropped her dishcloth and looked pleadingly at her mother. Her mother nodded her head. "Call in Mr. Pye," she said, referring to the way the men in Washington always spoke. "Call in Mr. Pye," they'd say whenever they got in a bird jam. This was not a bird jam. It was a dog jam and a dishwashing jam. But in this family it did not matter what sort of a jam it was. "Call in Mr. Pye" suited every occasion.

Papa and Grampa obligingly came in from the parlor, rolled up their shirt-sleeves and fell to on the dishes, meanwhile reminiscing about KP duty in the army. Rachel and Jerry grabbed their coats and hats from the rack by the door and hurried out of the house.

Mama followed them to the door. "I'm sure he is not far away," she told them, giving them both a good-luck hug and kiss. "Now. Hurry back before it gets too dark."

Somehow this made Rachel and Jerry want to cry. *Shucks,* thought Jerry. *He must be right around here somewhere.*

Still, neither one of the children said anything that might reassure the other. To both of them the possibility was too real that they might not find Ginger, that Ginger might be gone completely and forever. They both had an awful feeling that this might be so.

First they went to every yard in their block, and all around the square of the block. They whistled for him and they called, "Ginger, Ginger! Here pup, here pup!" But Ginger was not anywhere right around home, that was certain.

They buttoned their coats tighter and they went farther and farther, up one street and down another, whistling and calling all the time. It was a cold day, and a very fine snow—the first of winter—began to

fall. After a while a thin gossamer layer glistened everywhere, and it was cold and damp underfoot.

"He'll be cold," said Jerry. "Out all this time."

"Oh, Ginger," gasped Rachel, hardly able to bear it that they did not at least know where he was. She knew not to cry, though, because she was nine years old and children that age did not cry in Cranbury. She usually managed not to cry anymore when she felt like crying. Until now, when they couldn't find Ginger, the main times when she found it almost impossible not to cry were the times in school when an awfully sad story was being read out loud.

Evangeline was one of these awfully sad stories and sometimes Rachel had to press her fingers in her ears, trying not to hear. But she heard anyway and she would have to keep swallowing hard to keep from crying out loud and disgracing herself and all girls of nine in general. She would dry her tears on her petticoat under her desk, hoping it was supposed she had a cold.

Stories of old men also made her cry. There was the old man in *Hans Brinker*. And there was one dreadful story about an old man which the teacher in Room Four had read the class. The old man in this story was so feeble he spilled all his food on himself with his shaking hands. He made such a mess his family made him eat on a bench behind the kitchen stove while they ate somewhere else away from him. Rachel could hardly bear to think of that sad story ever. When Grampa got that old, she would make him eat right at the table with them all and slobber as much as he wanted. It was awful to be put on a bench behind the kitchen stove.

Dog stories, especially if there were cruelty involved, made her cry too. Consider the *Dog of Flanders!* Now, not to cry over not finding Ginger was even harder than not crying over the sad stories. And how could they ever go home without him?

"Ginger! Ginger pup!"

They went way over to parts of the town where they hardly ever went. It was growing dark because there was not daylight saving time anymore. The lonely lights in the houses, looking sad and shrunken in the deepening dusk, were coming on. And still the children plodded on, up one street and around a corner and down another street, and calling all the time, or whistling.

They had finally woven their way over to the part of town where Gramma lived. They were on Second Avenue, the street where, that first day when they had bought Ginger for one dollar, they had heard the mysterious footsteps. Maybe here they would find him. They called, "Ginger! Ginger!" and they whistled the seven short whistles with the uptilt on the last note, and they walked slowly, listening hard between calls and whistles. But they heard nothing, no little yelp or whine saying where their puppy was.

They began to knock at the doors of friendly looking houses. "Have you seen our dog?" they asked. "He's a little brown-and-white puppy."

No one had. They took a quick look in every

hall to see if the old felt hat was hanging there, the only clue they had. But they did not see it on any of the pegs they glimpsed.

One door that they knocked at happened to be the door of Wally Bullwinkle, the big boy in Jerry's class at school. He acted surprisingly unfriendly. Since the whole class was still talking about Jerry's smart dog, Ginger, and how he had climbed the fire escape, naturally Jerry and Rachel would have expected him to be very concerned about their dog's disappearance, or at least interested. They thought he might ask them in and talk the whole thing over with them, suggesting clues.

But they had hardly knocked at his door when it opened a tiny crack, as though Wally Bullwinkle had been right there waiting for them, and Wally whispered to them to get away from here. He said, still in a whisper, no, he had not seen their old dog; and furthermore, he said he had an enormous dog himself, and this dog was so ferocious Wally had to keep him locked up with heavy chains. So they better not come knocking at his door anymore, see?

Jerry and Rachel hurried away from there. "Maybe he did not have any Thanksgiving dinner," said Rachel, who was always ready to make excuses for anybody, even the unpleasantest people.

They recalled a story they had heard of a man over here, somewhere on Second Avenue, who had had his nose bitten off by a dog. Fortunately a bystander picked the nose up and stuck it back on this man's face where it belonged and, so the story went, held it there until the doctor arrived. The doctor sewed the nose back on, and it was only a little crooked. From then on the man was known as Bit-nose Ned.

Now Jerry and Rachel wondered. Supposing it was Wally Bullwinkle's dog that had done this. If so, it was kind of him, after all, to warn them. They'd better take his advice and stay away from this place. Their noses were so little, if they were bitten off, it would not be an easy matter to sew them back on.

Then Jerry said, "Pooh! I don't believe Wally has a dog at all. I never heard him say anything about having a dog. He's always boasting about something, that's all."

Rachel was silent. She was thinking that, if she was not careful, she might turn into a Wally Bullwinkle. Twice yesterday, twice on one day, she had said something that was not true. She wondered if the disappearance of Ginger Pye was punishment for saying these two things that were not true.

The first wrong thing she had said yesterday morning to Mrs. Carruthers when she was running home from school across the lot. Mrs. Carruthers had said to her, "Rachel," she had said. "I suppose you are having turkey for dinner tomorrow."

Rachel had said, "No. We aren't having turkey. But we are having *three* chickens."

Actually, she had been told they were going to

have two chickens, which seemed tremendous enough, but in comparison to a turkey, they were probably nothing in Mrs. Carruthers' estimation, so she had tacked one on. As it happened they had had three chickens after all, so the statement was not really untrue. Gramma said the two chickens she had chosen were not large enough and so she had brought another, as a surprise. However, at the time Rachel told Mrs. Carruthers about having *three*, she thought they were having *two*. Therefore it was a wrong thing to say, especially as she had been ashamed they were having chicken and not turkey. Yet, that was nothing to be ashamed of.

The other wrong thing she had said, she had said yesterday afternoon to Mrs. Stokes, the lady who had given the big ice cream party. It happened that Rachel and a girl named Muriel Jenks, who had curls and a coat trimmed with white bunny fur, were dancing on Rachel's front lawn and turning handsprings. Muriel Jenks went to Miss Chichester's dancing school and Muriel said, "Why don't you take dancing lessons?" And Rachel said, "I do. I go far far away and I take lessons from this teacher that is far far away." And all the while, of course, she didn't take dancing lessons at all.

This was not so bad, for Muriel would think this

was all a game of pretending and Muriel would like to imagine that Rachel had an interesting life somewhere of which she knew nothing. But unfortunately at this moment Mrs. Stokes came along—she always seemed to glide up the street, she was so graceful —and she said, "My, what fine little dancers. And where do you take lessons?" she had asked.

Muriel said, "Miss Chichester in Moose Hall."

Mrs. Stokes would have gone on then without asking any more questions, but Rachel just piped up and said, "And I take from a teacher that is different and she teaches far far away."

"That's why she dances that way, not my way," said Muriel.

Mrs. Stokes smiled and said that was fine, they both danced beautifully and they must come and dance for her daughter Nancy sometime. And then she went on up the street.

Rachel looked after Mrs. Stokes in dismay. Where had the words come from? The wrong words? She raced after Mrs. Stokes and she whispered to her, "Hey," she said. "I really don't take dancing lessons. I said I do. But I don't." And Mrs. Stokes had smiled and said what a very good joke that was. Rachel looked up at her gratefully and then had run back to Muriel who wanted to know what had been said. But Rachel didn't answer. Some other time she would tell Muriel about the dancing-school joke, not then.

Now. It was possible that these two wrong things she had said were changing her into a Wally Bullwinkle, and that in punishment Ginger was stolen from them. But that could not be, she reasoned hopefully, because, after all, Ginger was mostly Jerry's dog, and Jerry had not said the wrong things. Still, from now on, she would never say *three* when it was *two*. And she would not say she also went to dancing school when she didn't.

The snow flurry had stopped but the weather had turned awfully bleak and cold. When they cut across fields their feet crunched on the crisp little frost castles forming. They wiped their noses and they pressed their lips together to keep from sobbing. "Ginger! Ginger!" they gulped. In the end they had to go home without Ginger.

Their only hope now was that perhaps he had shown up at home and was right there all this time that they had been searching the town for him. This hope put speed in their tired toes and they tried to convince themselves that all this afternoon had been a bad dream from which they would awaken, and they would find everything as it always was at home with Ginger, perhaps, charging at the enemy dog in the pier glass mirror.

This was not so. They could tell it was not so the minute they got home because, if Ginger had been there, he would be racing to the door to meet them, the way he always did. Instead, it was awfully quiet in the house. Mama and Papa were sitting in the living room looking rather worried for they had been gone a long long time and it was nearly nine o'clock. Uncle Bennie and Gramma and Grampa

had not been able to wait for them any longer and had left. It was funny that Jerry and Rachel had not passed them, but they must have gone home by way of Hickory Street instead of Second Avenue where the children had last been, the street of the mysterious footstepper, and of Wally Bullwinkle and Bit-nose Ned.

Rachel and Jerry were too tired and too heavy-hearted to say anything or to eat anything, not even the warm milk Mama wanted them to have at least. They went upstairs to bed and they didn't say anything to each other and they climbed into their beds and neither one of them had the thought to play the Boombernickles story game, the game that they had played every other night for so long they could not remember when it had started. They just crawled into their beds in their own rooms and put their heads down under the covers and cried. In private one could cry. On an occasion like this, when they had lost their dog, they could certainly cry.

Jerry told himself how he had watched this certain puppy and wanted this puppy from when it was only a few days old; and how he had studied this puppy every day and been impressed with how sweet and smart he was; and how he had wondered where he would earn the dollar to buy him. He told himself how Sam Doody came to the rescue; how he earned the dollar, with the help of Rachel and Uncle Bennie, dusting the pews; how he had then bought the puppy with this dollar they had earned.

And Jerry told himself about the tricks he had taught Ginger, the smart dog he was. Ginger knew many tricks now. But Jerry was careful not to boast about him in front of Dick Badger or anybody, but especially not in front of Dick Badger, because Dick's dog, Duke, knew only the one trick—how to scratch his stomach when you scratched his back, a certain special place on his back. Ginger, on the other hand, when he was only about ten weeks old, had trailed Jerry to school and gone up the fire escape, even bringing a pencil Jerry had lost with him. Dick Badger's father ran the *Cranbury Chronicle* and he had put this story of Ginger on the fire escape in the newspaper, even running a picture of Ginger with a pencil in his mouth under the caption "Intellectual dog." The fellow who had also wanted to buy Ginger in the beginning must have seen the story and it probably made him wilder than ever to get hold of Ginger. Was it this same old fellow who had stolen Ginger, or who?

He'll be cold, thought Rachel, sobbing silently to herself.

The Cranbury Chronicle

EST. 1879   OcTober 13, 1919

Intellectual Dog of Jerry Pye.

School was in a hullabaloo over the arrival of Ginger Pye on the fire escape carrying his pencil with him.

Fire Department answers Three Calls Thursday

The Cranbury fire dep. was called out to three Thursday night. Two o originated from bu. Tresses.

Fireman Ben

He'll be wondering where I am, thought Jerry in anguish.

And they cried themselves to sleep. Jerry had a dream that Ginger Pye was asleep on his feet, the way he always slept. But in the morning, when he waked up, this fine dream was shattered. Because Ginger was certainly gone.

8

Searching for Ginger Pye

With the disappearance of Ginger Pye on Thanksgiving Day, the biggest search there ever was in Cranbury began. Friday, Saturday, and Sunday of the Thanksgiving weekend Jerry and Rachel covered the entire town looking for their puppy, calling him, and asking everybody they met if they had seen a dog such as they described.

"He's brown and white and has almost no tail, and he has elegant [they meant eloquent] eyes," they explained eagerly. And they said, "He answers to the name of Ginger, Ginger Pye, Ginger pup, or just pup, or puppy."

"What a great many names," said one lady, confused.

"It depends on how you say it, if he'll come," said Rachel. She envisioned a big class of Cranbury people learning how to call Ginger the right way, with affection and authority, and then of all these people going everywhere, calling and calling.

No one they asked had seen Ginger. They went up the country roads on the outskirts of the town, and they went along the shore, looking in all the little red boathouses. With their heels crunching on the wafer-thin ice, they made their way out to the end of Gooseneck Point to ask the lighthouse keeper if he had seen a little lost dog. He had not. They saw no trace of Ginger anywhere. It was as though the earth had swallowed him.

How had he got out of the yard? That was the puzzle. They decided that probably someone must have climbed over the fence—the fence, no doubt, that bordered the side street and where Uncle Bennie had seen the hat that first Sunday they had had Ginger. The person may have tempted Ginger with a piece of candy. Then he may have thrown a coat over Ginger and clamped his jaws together so he could not make a sound. Ginger may have whimpered but the Pyes would not have heard because of all the eating of drumsticks, and the laughter, and the conversation. He must have been stolen while dinner was going on. The thief must have plotted this from the beginning—to steal Ginger Pye while Thanksgiving dinner was going on.

"Edgar," Mama said to Papa. "I told you some time ago there seems to have been some sort of unsavory character around."

"I know it, Lucy," said Papa, looking troubled and hurt and running his fine hand through his thin red hair. He could not understand how anyone could steal a pet belonging to a child. He just could not understand it, and he stomped through the house shaking his head sternly.

Jerry could understand it. Everybody in the whole town, almost, knew about Ginger on the fire escape and made comments on the intellectual dog, because they had read the story in the *Cranbury Chronicle*. Not many extraordinary events happened in Cranbury and when one did, the ins and outs of it were naturally discussed at length and for many many days. Even the teacher in Jerry's class got over being angry about the hullabaloo when she read the story in the paper and read her name there and found she, too, was famous. Probably the unsavory character had read the story of Ginger on the fire escape and this made him decide once and for all to get hold of the brilliant puppy.

It would be hard to say why all the Pyes thought the unsavory character was a man, and not a woman, a boy, or a girl, for no one had ever really seen him.

They had heard his footsteps, and they had seen his hat on four occasions. Since his old felt hat looked like the hat of a man, naturally they just reached the conclusion that the unsavory character was a man, without even considering the other possibilities.

This shows that the Pyes were not good detectives, but none of them ever for one minute thought of themselves as detectives. Mr. Pye thought of himself as a bird man and a father, Mrs. Pye as a mother and a housewife, Jerry as a rock man and a boy, and Rachel as a bird man and a girl. There was not a detective among them. There wasn't even a detective in the whole town of Cranbury for that matter, but there was a Chief of Police named Mr. Larrimer, and they intended to speak to him.

First, however, it was sensible to ask Mrs. Speedy, who was out of the hospital now, to try and rack her brains a little and see if she could remember what the other person looked like who had wanted to buy Ginger in the first place. This they did before they went to the Chief of Police.

In spite of none of them being detectives this was a very astute step for the Pyes to take. After all, Mrs. Speedy was the only person who had ever really seen the unsavory character, that is if *that* person who had wanted Ginger and waved the dollar at her and *this* person who had stolen Ginger were one and the same. That, of course, they did not and would not know, but they all had the feeling they were the same.

So the Pyes went to Mrs. Speedy, and she said so many people came to her dairy for eggs or milk or butter or, perhaps, to buy a chicken, and last August was such a long time away, you bet, that she couldn't say whether it was man, woman, or child; and she wouldn't want to get the innocent in trouble, you bet. She said, if it ever got to the point where women served on the jury, she would always say, "Innocent." You bet. Moreover, she was awfully absentminded, and had had that stroke, so she could not walk or talk awfully well; and it was a wonder, considering she was also a little deaf and did not see too well either, that she remembered Ginger and Jerry after all these months, let alone remembering what the other party looked like. No, she could not recollect that other person, but it was a shame Ginger was gone. "A shame, you bet," she said. But then, as they were leaving, she said, "I remember now. That person had a curious hat on —it seems to me it was on the yellow. Yes. On the yellow, you bet."

The Pyes thanked her gratefully. They appreciated the interest she had shown and the description of the hat, but they knew no more than in the beginning.

Anyway, it was undoubtedly because of the hat that Jerry and Rachel, and, in fact, all of them, had it firmly fixed in their minds that the unsavory character was a man. Rachel and Jerry were so sure of this they drew a picture of him, imagining what the horrid person looked like. The picture they drew of the man was on the order of the slick villains in the moving pictures, with a black mustache. Once the picture was drawn that way, they could not think of him as looking any different. When they went with Mr. Pye to Chief Larrimer, they brought the original drawing with them, to help him spot the man.

While they were waiting to see Chief Larrimer —there was no one ahead of them but Chief Larrimer always kept people waiting to give the appearance of being terribly busy—Rachel and Jerry examined the criminals' roster posted on the bulletin board in the Town Hall. They wanted to see if any of these criminals looked the way they had drawn Unsavory. After a careful comparison they decided there was no one like their villain. Anyway the criminals in this roster were not Cranbury criminals because, until now, there were no Cranbury criminals. These, whose pictures were in the Town Hall, were nationwide criminals who held up trains and made fake money and committed such crimes. They were hardly the sort of man Unsavory was who stole just dogs.

When they finally got to see Chief Larrimer, and Jerry had shown him the unsavory character's picture, the policeman was very interested and said Jerry and Rachel should go to art school. They told him the whole story, bringing in about the mysterious footsteps and Mrs. Speedy and the yellow felt hat.

Chief Larrimer said he knew of no such char*ackt*er, but he would be on the lookout. Chief Larrimer was a new and young Chief of Police, having succeeded the recently retired and notable Cranbury citizen, Chief Mulligan. He was anxious to do a good job and now he swung his little-used stick in a high dido, indicating he meant business.

Jerry said, "Sir," and then he realized he should have said, "Chief," so he started again, and his words came out, "Sir chief," which sounded odd, but he went on nevertheless. "Sir chief," he said. "If you find a man with that sort of a hat, you can tell whether it is our man or not because the hat of

our man will have a red crayon mark inside the band where Dick Badger marked it up at the res', and the hats of the innocent will not."

Chief Larrimer twirled his billy stick. "If he marked his hat," he said, "why didn't he turn the man over to me so I could jail him?"

When it was explained that they had seen only the hat and not the man, himself, Chief Larrimer was very interested. He was more impressed than ever that Rachel and Jerry had had the sense to draw a picture of him since they had seen only his hat. He wished that the people who came and complained to him about people stealing their chickens had one-half the sense.

The children then gave Chief Larrimer one of their clippings from the *Cranbury Chronicle* with Ginger's picture, labeled "Intellectual dog," and the story of him on the fire escape. The Chief remembered having read the story. "I thought at the time," he said, chuckling, "what kind of a breed of a dog is that? Intellectual dog." He thumbtacked the drawing and the clipping on the bulletin board and they looked impressive.

"Well," he said. He obviously meant they could all go now. "I pick up stray dogs now and then," he said. "Next time I pick one up, and no one claims it, I'll give it to you."

He meant this kindly but Jerry gulped and said, "No, thanks." After all, it was Ginger he wanted and not some other dog.

Now, having told Chief Larrimer, there was nothing for the Pyes to do but continue the search and hope the Chief was searching too, in places they would not know about.

On the way home from the Town Hall they happened to meet Sam Doody. They told him about the losing of Ginger Pye and he was very angry. "If I ever catch the fellow who stole your dog, I'll thrash the living daylights out of him," he said. He was still grinning, because Sam Doody was always grinning, but there was an angry glint in his eye. He promised to look over all tall fences and to keep an eye out everywhere he went. He was especially interested when Rachel told him it was the dollar he had given Jerry for dusting the pews that had bought Ginger in the first place.

Dick Badger's father ran an ad, free, every day for two weeks in the "lost and found" column of the *Cranbury Chronicle*. But nothing came of this.

They should run it in the headlines, not in the small lost and found type, thought Jerry. Naturally, since the ads were free, he said nothing.

Uncle Bennie was almost inconsolable. "Ginger back yet?" he asked every Saturday when he came to lunch.

Everyone shook his head, too heavyhearted to say anything.

Uncle Bennie saw that Jerry and Rachel felt very badly. Halfheartedly, knowing it would not compensate, he offered them his bubbah. "Ginger come back soon," he promised them, to make them feel better. And he added importantly, "Uncle Bennie find Ginger. I find."

Many children in Cranbury helped Jerry and Rachel search for Ginger, the dog with the pencil. Sometimes they met at the flagpole on the Green and separated, going in six different directions, trusting one was bound to be right, some racing, some crying, "I know just where to look."

Most often Dick Badger joined in the searching. Duke was told to stick his nose to the ground and behave like a bloodhound. Duke behaved like a bloodhound, but he didn't find Ginger. He found only a great many peculiar objects which he brought

to Dick and laid at his feet, hoping wistfully that these were what was meant by the earnest pleading. He even scratched his stomach without anyone scratching his back but apparently this did not do either.

Sometimes Rachel and her friend, Addie Egan, went searching on their own.

"I never knew we'd meet a vilyun in real life," said Rachel to Addie Egan one day, when they were off searching. "Only in books."

"A what?" asked Addie Egan respectfully. Her admiration for her best friend was boundless, but she had never heard the expression.

"A vilyun," said Rachel patiently.

"Oh," said Addie thoughtfully. Then rather hesitantly, for it did not seem good policy to correct her defender—and everybody would still be saying she had cooties, and even calling her "Cooty," if it had not been for Rachel—she said, "I thought the word was pronounced 'villun.' "

"No," said Rachel confidently. "It's vilyun. Like million."

"I think it's villun," said Addie Egan bravely.

"No," said Rachel. "Vilyun. It must be vilyun because vilyun sounds more vilyunous than villun, the way you say it."

Rachel Pye liked words. Sometimes, however, she attached the wrong meaning to a word. For instance, the word *detestable*. She thought detestable meant "awfully nice." It just sounded like another way of saying "awfully nice" to her. For a time she had had the habit of saying "Detestable" to everybody who came to the house, especially to Miss Meadow, who gave Jerry lessons on the piano.

"Hello, Detestable," Rachel would greet Miss Meadow affectionately, not understanding why Mama and Miss Meadow always laughed.

After a while Mama explained the true meaning of the word to Rachel. *Detestable* meant "horrid" and not "awfully nice" at all. At first Rachel could not believe it, *detestable* sounded so nice to her. Then, when she was convinced, she was appalled. She really liked Miss Meadow and what could she be thinking, being called "Detestable" the minute she put her head in the door? But Miss Meadow seemed to consider the nickname funny and took no offense.

However, to make amends, Mama suggested that Rachel give Miss Meadow a very sweet little gilt vanity case which Rachel had got from the grocery store from saving coffee coupons. Rachel had meant to keep pennies in it for it was just the right size for pennies and had, moreover, a little gilt chain attached to it. At the end of the chain was a little ring. You could wear it on your finger.

But Mama said she should give the vanity case to Miss Meadow. Rachel was too young for vanities anyway, she said. So Rachel had. Miss Meadow was delighted and filled it up with talcum powder instead of pennies. She hadn't caught on to the idea it would be marvelous for pennies, and Rachel did miss the pretty little case. She then, at Mama's suggestion, tried switching her greeting from "Hello, Detestable," to "Hello, Adorable," but it never sounded as good and soon she dropped everything but the hello.

Now Addie Egan might possibly be right about the word being villun and not vilyun; but Rachel certainly hoped she was wrong in view of the fact that vilyun just simply sounded a great deal better. She graciously said, "We'll look it up in the dictionary and then you'll see. It's vilyun, vilyunous."

And off they went, up one street and down another, calling, "Ginger! Ginger!"

Although, at first, a very great many children helped Rachel and Jerry hunt for Ginger Pye, after a while they grew tired of the same old search. Though they all promised to keep their eyes open for the man whose picture they had examined at the Town Hall, and his hat which Jerry described, one by one they dropped off. Then, only Jerry and Rachel looked, either together or by themselves. They never got any clues as to where their puppy might be, but they never gave up hope.

"Too many people know about the funny hat," said Jerry. "Naturally he won't wear it anymore—the unsavory character," said Jerry, giving character the same pronunciation the Chief of Police had—char*ackt*er.

"Oh-h-h," exclaimed Rachel, almost over-whelmed at Jerry's smartness in figuring this out.

In the evening, now, Jerry and Rachel had a new game they played. They drew their own funny papers, dividing a sheet of paper into four or six little squares for the pictures and the captions. And they always had, as the villain, the man, the un-savory character as they had pictured him in the original drawing, the person who had stolen their dog, Ginger.

Although Jerry and Rachel never said this out loud, they had a silent mutual agreement that the wonderful nighttime adventures of Martin Boom-bernickles would not be continued ever again, not until the return of Ginger Pye.

It was hard, as the days went by and no sign or trace of Ginger appeared, for them to keep on hoping that he would return. But they did hope this and so

did Uncle Bennie. Uncle Bennie solemnly assured them over and over that he would find Puppy for them.

Whenever any of them thought of Ginger coming running back, they thought of him as the little puppy he was when he disappeared. They forgot that he would grow. Meanwhile, they called, "Ginger! Ginger!" all over the place.

9

Skeleton Houses

Skeleton houses are not, as some people might suppose, houses chuck-full of skeletons. They are new houses being built and at that stage where only the wooden framework has been erected.

When the wood was getting low in the woodbin, Rachel and Jerry would listen for the sound of hammering and pounding echoing through the cold quiet of a winter day in Cranbury, telling them a new house was being built. Then off they would go with their express wagon or their sleds to the skeleton house and pile these high with chunks of brand-new wood to start the fire in the kitchen range.

This was turning out to be a very cold winter, but so far, and it was almost Christmas, there had been very little snow. It was so cold for a few days that the harbor froze over entirely, something that had happened only once before that Mama could remember. It was very exciting and, if you wanted, you could get from Cranbury to the city by ice boat. "It's like Holland!" yelled Rachel delightedly when she looked out of Papa's high tower window one day and saw, in the distance, ice boats the boys had made sailing swiftly over the harbor.

Keeping the woodbin full was Jerry and Rachel's special job. What was the sense of buying wood when, with a little ingenuity, plenty of it could be found? Ordinarily Jerry and Rachel were able to keep the woodbin filled with driftwood gathered along the shore. But now, with all the ice in the harbor, naturally there was no wood drifting in and they had to think of other places to find it. Next to the shore, the most important place for finding kindling was in skeleton houses. Because there had been so little snow, building on the new houses had not stopped and the woodbin was almost never empty.

The children always went to the skeleton houses after the carpenters had left, or on Saturdays and Sundays, in order not to be in the way. Naturally the children did not take great big pieces of wood, only small pieces of plank and shavings and the carpenters were happy to have these cleared away. They had wonderful times in the skeleton houses, climbing all over them, even up to the second floor that was not yet a floor at all, but merely great beams stretched across where the floor was going to be. They were such good climbers they never fell down and broke a leg or anything.

However, when a new house reached the plastering stage they could no longer go in. They used to go in the plastered houses, too, but in one of

these Rachel had rubbed against the wet plaster and had practically ruined her coat. This was a brand-new bright red coat that Mama had made for her and the plaster turned the red to orange in spots. It looked awful. Mama did not scold, but then, Mama never scolded. However, she did suggest that here-after, when a skeleton house was in the plastering stage, they'd better not go inside of it, just stay on the outside. Staying on the outside was not such fun but they stuck to the rule and went only into skeleton houses that had not the plaster in them yet. And so they ruined no more coats.

One cold evening Rachel and Jerry went to a skeleton house way over on Second Avenue, the street of Wally Bullwinkle and the mysterious foot-stepper. Even though the plastering had not been begun on this skeleton house, since it was dark they naturally did not go inside lest they slip off a beam into the deep and dank cellar. Instead they stumbled around in the dark where the porch was going to be. They had very good pickings that night for they had got here before anyone else, even before the Moffats who also knew about skeleton houses for wood, and who, ordinarily, were first on the scene. They soon had their wagon loaded high.

On these trips to skeleton houses they always

kept their eyes open for signs of Ginger Pye, and still kept calling him. They were always thinking of Ginger, and speaking of him, and remembering him. Even though it was almost Christmas they were not likely to forget their puppy, especially Jerry, whose particular pet Ginger Pye was.

Rachel was not likely to forget either since she had about the best memory of anybody in the whole Pye family. Rachel remembered things that happened before she was two. She remembered the house they had lived in when she was about one that was near the railroad tracks. And she remembered the trains, New York to Boston, streaking past with a sudden roar. She also remembered about Aletta Livingston who had lived next door to them in that house. Aletta was also about one year old and she always looked out of her window at Rachel when Rachel looked out of hers at Aletta.

Of course, with a memory like that, Rachel would not be likely to forget about Ginger ever; and now, as they were tying a rope around their wood to keep it steady, and drawing on their mittens, she said, "Remember, Jerry? This is just about where we first heard the mysterious footsteps."

Naturally Jerry remembered this too, though he didn't remember anything before he was two, the

way Rachel did. In fact, a lady had once asked him what was the first thing he remembered and he said he didn't know he was alive until he was five.

Now, ready to leave for home, the children stood silently for a moment. It was strange how, whenever they were in this part of Cranbury, they thought most keenly about Ginger. Perhaps this was because of the memory of the footsteps. Anyway it really seemed to them that they might be nearer Ginger here than anywhere else. In spite of Wally Bullwinkle's warning to stay away from here, and the memory of Bit-nose Ned, they came and called and searched up and down Second Avenue more than any other street in town.

They were very lucky that this new skeleton house was going up over here where, somehow, they felt nearest to Ginger. They could pay frequent visits to the new house, and Wally Bullwinkle, as well as all the other people who lived over here, would not wonder at seeing them around so often. All these people would see and hear the new house being built. They would see Rachel and Jerry. They would see the wagon full of shavings and wood, and they would think it was natural that, at the same time as getting wood, the children would try to find their dog all over again. These people and Wally would realize that you don't look once for a lost dog and then give up and never look or call again.

Yes. The new house gave them an excellent excuse to knock on doors over here all over again asking people about Ginger. However, they would try to avoid, not only Wally's door, but also the door of a certain lady they called "Mincemeat."

One night when Jerry and Rachel had been desperately knocking on doors asking people had they seen Ginger, a woman came to the door and before they could even get out the sentence about Ginger she held up her hands and said, "I'm making mincemeat. Can't you see I'm making mincemeat?" And she slammed the door in their faces. Her hands hadn't had any mincemeat on them that they could see, but the way she held them up and the way she said, "mincemeat," made them imagine they were just dripping with it. So they called her "Mincemeat" from then on.

One reason that they kept knocking at doors asking people if they had seen Ginger was that they hoped to glimpse the old yellow hat hanging on a peg in a hallway. Of course they could not be positive that the person who had stolen Ginger had anything to do with the person in the old felt hat or the mysterious footsteps. But, lacking any other clues, they persisted in thinking so.

Well, now their wood was all loaded and their mittens on and their overcoats buttoned up tight, and still they stood and listened in the vast dark night. The wonderful smell of new wood was in their nostrils and also the dank smell of black earth from the cellar recently dug.

Often, on Ginger-searching expeditions Rachel and Jerry stood still as mice. Naturally, if they made a lot of noise and called every minute, how would they be able to hear Ginger when he barked or whined, letting them know where he was? This was one of their listening periods. In fact, this whole trip was more of a listening than a calling trip. It was so quiet they would have felt funny breaking the quietness with their voices. It would be as though the world would shake in half if they called just once. Their ears rang with the quiet.

Then, in the quiet, Jerry thought he heard a dog yelping. But at the same moment, Rachel, because the stillness was making her feel spooky, to break the spell, called suddenly, "Here, Ginger, Ginger, Ginger! Here, Ginger pup!" And Jerry heard the dog no more.

"Sh-sh-sh," said Jerry, grabbing Rachel's arm. "I thought I heard a dog yelping. It could have been Ginger. It didn't sound far away either."

There was no more yelping, however, and though

they called and whistled and coaxed till they were hoarse, and then listened hard, nothing but stillness answered them. Jerry didn't even know from what direction the bark had come. Cold and downcast they carefully, not to spill any, lugged their wagonload of wood out of the lumpy yard of the new skeleton house.

Then, as they turned onto the sidewalk, in the dark, whom should they encounter but the man in the yellow hat! They could not help gasping in terror and surprise. But wait! On second sight they saw it was not *their* man in the yellow hat at all. It was just Wally Bullwinkle, the boy in Jerry's class, and he simply had the same sort of hat as Unsavory, that was all. Oh, they were relieved. This was not *their* unsavory character that they had drawn the picture of and posted in the rogue's gallery at the Town Hall and put in their funny papers as the villain. This was only Wally Bullwinkle, the owner of a dog as ferocious as the one they had heard about that had bit the nose off Bit-nose Ned.

Wally stood in their path and Jerry and Rachel smiled at him, they were so glad to see him and not the real Unsavory. No, they would not care to encounter the real Unsavory all by themselves over here on Second Avenue even though they were fairly

near a streetlamp and not an awfully long way from the house of Judge Ball, the most important man in Cranbury. It would be hard to think of a more important man than Judge Ball in Cranbury and they had dusted his pew once whether he knew it or not.

Wally did not seem as glad to see them as they were to see him. He did not return their smile. And then on third sight, they saw that Wally didn't have a yellow hat on after all. He had no hat on. He was bareheaded. Were they just so eager to see the yellow hat they had begun imagining they saw yellow hats all over the place? That's what they wondered.

Wally snarled, "What are you doing over here? What are you snooping around for over here anyway? Didn't I tell you I'd sick my hound on you if I ever caught you over here?"

"We're not snooping. We're getting wood and we're looking for our dog," said Rachel indignantly.

Jerry clenched his fists. He was not the sort of boy to ever say ouch and now he was trying to remember the one, two, threes of self-protection that tall Sam Doody had taught him. It looked as though he might have to put his knowledge into effect for the first time on Wally Bullwinkle.

But Wally did not give Jerry a chance even to warm up. He gave their wood a good kick so they would have to gather it and pile it up again, and then he raced off toward his house a few doors up the street. He was gone.

"He's mean," said Rachel as they stacked the new wood up again.

Jerry said nothing. He couldn't understand what had got into Wally. What'd he have to act like this for? That was what Jerry wondered.

"I thought he had a yellow hat on, when I first saw him," said Jerry.

"I did, too," said Rachel.

"But he didn't have a hat on at all," said Jerry.

"Unless he threw it in the bushes," said Rachel.

"I didn't see him flip it off or pick it up or anything," said Jerry, puzzled.

"You know what?" said Rachel. "I think there is a secret society of mean people that wear funny yellow hats. Unsavory is one and perhaps is the head man. And Wally Bullwinkle makes two. There may be others."

"Jiminy crickets," said Jerry, appalled at the prospect. "Still," he said, "we will always know our yellow hat from all others because of the mark Dick Badger put in it."

"Yes," said Rachel. "Unless, as in *The Tinder Box*, the mean people with the yellow hats have the sense to put red marks in all of them. The way to tell have they done this or not is for you to look in Wally's hat, if he ever wears it to school and hangs it on the peg. If he has a yellow hat, that is. If his yellow hat has a red mark in it, you will know all the yellow-hat people have done the same thing, put red marks in their hats, to throw us off the track. But you can try to get it out of Wally who the head man, Unsavory, is."

"Oh," said Jerry tiredly. "That's fairy-tale stuff." He was remembering the poison tomatoes and Rachel's unreasonable reasonableness and he was reminding himself, the earnest way she was talking, he should be on guard.

As they turned down Second Avenue, starting for home, a little terrier, black-and-white and full-grown, came running out of a yard barking at them. No doubt this was the dog Jerry had heard before, they thought dolefully. Probably here they were, spending all their time looking for Ginger over in this part of town, when all the while he might be over in a completely different section. Hereafter they would think of new and far places to go and search.

"You know," said Rachel. "Ginger came to be a member of the family on Labor Day, or just before Labor Day anyway. He found you in school the day before Columbus Day. He was stolen on Thanksgiving Day. Maybe he will come home on Christmas Day. Maybe he is a sort of a holiday dog."

"M-m-m," said Jerry. Christmas was not very far away. But it was too far to consider Ginger being gone all that time more. In silence they left the skeleton house far behind and went home with their wood, their breath blowing behind them in gusts in the crisp fresh wind that had arisen. The wind, at any rate, broke the silence and sent dry boughs creaking and bending and the sign in front of the drugstore swaying and rocking on its hinges.

There might be something in what Rachel said, a holiday dog, thought Jerry. He could see no catch in that. *He might come home for Christmas. He might.*

When they reached home they got out one of their drawings of Unsavory, the villain. They had colored his hat yellow as they did in all the pictures. Now they wished the person they had seen tonight had been the real villain instead of Wally, just a boy in Jerry's class. If it had been Unsavory, they might have their puppy back by now. To think there was more than one yellow hat of this sort in town! If Wally had had a yellow hat on, that is, and it wasn't a case of their just having yellow hats on the brain. Then they would have one less clue. In fact the only clue they would have left then, aside from their drawing, was the red mark Dick Badger had put in the real hat. Even at that, Wally might have been playing around at the res' that day and Dick might have put the red mark in his hat and not in that of Unsavory at all.

Well, as Rachel had suggested, the way to tell whether it had been Wally and not the real Unsavory at the res', was for Jerry, the first chance he got, to examine Wally's yellow hat—if Wally did have a yellow hat, that is, and it was not a case of hats on the brain tonight.

That was what they decided to do, they told one another, as they got out their papers and pencils and crayons, pushed everything off the square dining room table, and began to draw a new funny paper of the unsavory character. In this one, they had him being the head man of a band of yellow-hat mean men, as Rachel had suggested he might be, and in the distance the Secret Service men were coming.

10

The Giant Steps

Wally never wore any hat to school except an old brown worsted one. "We must have had yellow hats on the brain that night at the skeleton house," said Jerry to Rachel.

"Yes," said Rachel. "Hats on the brain."

Ginger didn't come home for Christmas, and he didn't come home for New Year's, nor for Lincoln's Birthday, nor Washington's Birthday either. If he were a holiday dog, that is a dog for whom important events happened chiefly on holidays, he would have to come home for Easter, Decoration Day, or the Fourth of July. There were not many holidays left in the year.

Now it was the beginning of the Easter vacation. Spring was in the air. Crocuses were coming up and the trees looked ready to bud. Spring, in fact, would burst forth at any moment. What fine trips Jerry and

Ginger Pye could be having, now the weather was fine. They could go, not only up to the res' and down to the beach. They could go up East Rock and West Rock and the Sleeping Giant, too.

But Ginger did not come home on Easter and on Monday after Easter, with the house full of fragrant hyacinths, lilies, and tulips, Jerry sat on a stool in the kitchen eating an apple and thinking. He was thinking—here Ginger Pye had found Jerry in the classroom when he was only a little puppy. Yet he, Jerry, couldn't find Ginger, though he was a boy ten years old. And it was not that he didn't think of unusual places to look either. He even looked in the movies.

Whenever Jerry went to the moving pictures, which was usually once a week on Saturday afternoons to see the adventures of Stingaree, he would get a terrific feeling of loneliness if he saw a dog on the screen. The thought had occurred to him that, since Ginger was such a smart dog, some talent scout might have snatched him up and made off with him; and perhaps that was what the man in the yellow hat was, a talent scout now far away in Hollywood with Ginger. Jerry studied all dogs in movies but, so far, none was Ginger.

Rachel sat by the stove. She was watching Jerry

eat his apple for Jerry had a way of eating an apple that was altogether different from the way she, or Addie Egan, or anybody else she knew ate apples.

Jerry always carried a jackknife around with him. Usually the jackknife had one half of its bone handle missing, but it cut very well anyway. Her brother always carefully peeled his apple with his jackknife and ate it in neat chunks that he cut off with his knife. Rachel enjoyed the ceremonious, crisp, clean manner of Jerry's apple eating.

Jerry had also first called Rachel's attention to apple sandwiches. "They are very good," he said.

"An apple sandwich?" asked Rachel in surprise. The image of a large apple in its natural state, bulging between two thin slices of bread, had flashed before her eyes.

"No, foolish," said her brother. And slicing his apple in his same ceremonious way, he had put these crisp slices between two well-buttered slices of bread. He had invited Rachel to have a bite, a *small* bite, and it *was* good. But then, that was when Rachel had been at an age when alphabet soup, animal crackers, two yolks in the egg, watching her mother spell *Rachel* in Karo syrup on a piece of bread and butter or on a pancake, were all wonders setting her pondering for a long long time. Well, she still liked all these things, and she particularly enjoyed watching Jerry eating his apple in his special and tidy fashion, as he was doing now.

Jerry said, "I'd like to climb East Rock today." He had it in mind to look for Ginger in far places now. He was tired of looking just in Cranbury.

Rachel said, "So would I."

Jerry said, "Mama. Can we climb East Rock today with Dick Badger and Duke?"

"No," said Mama. "You are all too little to go up there alone."

"We can't ever go anywhere," said Jerry.

"That is nonsense," said Mama, going on with her typing of Papa's latest treatise on birds.

It was nonsense, so Jerry saw no use saying any more. Just then tall Sam Doody came in. He had several pots of geraniums—pink and red ones—in his arms; and he said, here, they could have these because, even after the sick and the hospitals had been taken care of, there had been a few left over at the church. The minister had told him to divide them up between himself, the altar guild, the sexton, and the curate, and who else deserved a few if not Jerry and Rachel Pye, his assistants?

Then Sam Doody said, "I was thinking of going up East Rock today." You would think Sam Doody was a thought reader, a mind reader, a clairvoyant, because that was exactly what Jerry and Rachel had been thinking of. "I have a new camera," he said. "And I want to get some shots. There's a little zoo up there. Did you know that?"

No, Jerry and Rachel had not known that. They just knew that there was this enormous rock called East Rock, and that they had never been up it. Trees grew on the top of East Rock and on three sides of it. But the face itself was nearly four hundred feet high, bare, bald, hard, and copper-colored.

They had seen East Rock from the trolley and

from the train going to Boston, but they had never been up it all the time they lived in Cranbury, which was all their lives. They had never been up West Rock either, a rock very similar on the other side of the city. West Rock had a cave on it, Judges Cave, and they had never been in it either. If Sam Doody took them up East Rock today, he might some other time take them up West Rock, too, to see the cave.

Jerry and Rachel looked at Mama. Surely she would let them go with tall Sam Doody so he could take some shots from up there? And surely Mama did. She even made some sandwiches for them all in a hurry, because after such a climb as going up the Giant Steps, they would certainly be very hungry.

"Giant Steps!" thought Rachel. That sounded the best of all. She asked no questions, for the minute she heard the expression, "Giant Steps," she had already figured out in her mind what they would be like. They would be enormous steps built by and for giants, the biggest steps anyone anywhere could imagine. Could she get up them? She bet she could.

Sam Doody, besides being the tallest boy in Cranbury, had the whitest teeth and the blackest hair, and he was always smiling. Even when he was just walking along, thinking, he looked as though he was smiling. In addition to being the captain of the high school basketball team, and the boy who kept the church in order, and scout, first class, he had, also, a father who looked like Woodrow Wilson. Besides all this, he took pictures that sometimes won prizes in camera contests. Jerry and Rachel were honored to be asked to go off with him on a picture-taking expedition. They climbed into his old jalopy and off they went, saying nothing in order not to interrupt Sam Doody in his thoughts.

Rachel and Jerry had not often been for rides in automobiles. Mr. Pye did not own one, for two reasons. He could not afford one. And he was not of a mechanical mind.

Grampa had an old Ford somewhat on the order of Sam Doody's jalopy, but riding with Grampa was such a breathtaking experience they did not enjoy it. The sensation was more like that of riding the Whip at Plum Beach than of a pleasant outing in an automobile enjoying the scenery. For instance, Grampa was apt to drive too close to the other side of the road. On one long trip, to visit a soldier cousin at Camp Niantic, going across a bridge, he had nearly deposited them all in the Connecticut River. So it seemed anyway from where Rachel and Jerry

sat in the front seat, and they courteously said, "No, thanks," when Grampa asked them if they would like to go for a ride.

"When Grampa gets really old and drooling I will go with him not to hurt his feelings," Rachel promised herself. But so far Grampa was such a young grampa it was still all right to say no thanks to something he suggested. Anyway he was just learning to drive. When he got the hang of it better they would go with him.

So now, off they went with a sputter and a bang and they sputtered and banged all the way out of town, through the city, and out to East Rock. Sam Doody drove on the right side of the road and it was a lovely ride. Sam parked his car near the foot of the great rock and they all got out, Rachel carrying the little bag of sandwiches. Since they were already hungry they ate these. This was a good idea for now they would not be encumbered with them climbing the Rock.

Jerry had no doubt but that they were to scale the face of the Rock, which is certainly what he wanted to do. Rachel, on the other hand, had no doubt they would go up by way of the Giant Steps, wherever they were. Naturally neither one of them would make a suggestion to Sam Doody.

They were standing at the base of the sheer face of the Rock now, looking up. Standing here, they could scarcely see the top. It looked as high and as slippery as the glass hill on top of which the princess lived. Since Jerry was a boy interested in rocks, he, of course, picked up some very interesting specimens and soon his pockets bulged with trap rock.

Sam was studying the Rock. He had a way of breathing through his smiling mouth and it was a comfortable sound to hear, Sam's breathing, like an audible smile. Would he take some shots here? the children wondered, and waited respectfully. But then Sam said, "Well, let's get going." And he strode up the road to the right.

Jerry could see that climbing the face of the Rock was not in the program. Quickly he said, "Ever climb the face of this Rock, Sam?"

"Well, not the face right in the middle where it is the sheerest, but on the edge, sort of, where there's sapling or a bush to grab hold of."

"That must be fun, too," said Jerry quickly. After all, the side of the face was almost as perilous as the middle of it, he thought.

"That the way you'd like to go up?" asked Sam Doody.

Jerry nodded, too happy to say anything.

"You, too?" asked Sam Doody of Rachel.

Rachel nodded courageously. It would be interesting, she assured herself, to scale East Rock, and she hoped to find an owl in its eyrie and tell Papa. "Dear Papa," her mind began the letter. "We climbed East Rock with Sam Doody and I saw an owl in its eyrie." That's what she would write Papa. She would be like Papa on Mount Pisgah. The Giant Steps would have to wait for next time, though of course it was a disappointment not to see these. She thought if they went up the face they would likewise come down it.

Jerry had to empty out his pockets of all the heavy rocks he had gathered. He hid them under a laurel bush and then, up they started. At first the going was easy because there were shrubs and small saplings trying persistently to grow in the Rock that they could cling to. But presently there was nothing but the beautiful copper-colored Rock itself and they had to feel with their fingers and grip with their knees and toes. It was the biggest climb that Jerry or Rachel had ever undertaken. They were both enjoying themselves and they felt very exhilarated. They went in this order: Jerry first, then Sam Doody, then Rachel. Soon Jerry was way above the others.

"Slow up there, fellow," said Sam Doody.

I'll have to hurry, thought Rachel. *Not to slow them up too much*. So she hurried. She was not the least bit afraid and she laughed to herself thinking of a certain time when she *had* been afraid on a high place. And that high place had been nowhere near as high as this.

That time, she and Jerry and Dick Badger had been climbing up onto Dick Badger's barn and jumping off onto a pile of old hay. They had done this over and over, taking turns, Dick first, then Jerry, then she, with no pauses or intermissions. Up, down, up, down, over and over. Suddenly at her turn to jump, Rachel's feet seemed to take root in the tar-papered roof. After all the jumps she had taken, for no reason she could think of, she simply could not jump again.

"Jump," said Dick. He had nearly bumped into her and knocked her off, the game, until now, had been going so rhythmically. "Jump," he said.

"Jump," urged Jerry. "You're holding us up."

How could Jerry and Dick jump with her standing there as though ready for the dive but not diving? At last, ashamed, she had moved over to the corner. She watched Dick and Jerry jump over and over again with no waits between. They paid no attention to her and she sat miserably on the corner banging her heels against the barn, watching the fearless ones.

At last she stood up and went over to the jumping spot. Now she would jump, she decided. But still she could not jump. She had to move aside again for the boys. And then they had had enough.

"C'mon, Rachel," called Jerry. "I'm getting hungry." He and Dick disappeared. But Jerry came back alone in a second. "Hey, Rache," he said. "Shall I get the ladder?"

"No," said Rachel. If she were to get down she must get down by herself or be a coward the rest of her born days. She must jump like she had a million times already.

Rachel sat on, in a sort of mesmerized misery. Dick's big dog, Duke, came out of the house and he looked up at her mournfully and curiously, sniffing gently. Then he went into his doghouse for his afternoon nap. From her high place she saw Dick and Jerry going off up the street together. They didn't even look to see if she were still up on the roof.

Finally, she stood up and she went over to the edge of the roof and without any more standing and trembling and "Oh, I can'ts" or anything, she jumped. She just jumped the way she had been doing before. And she went home and she never went up on that roof again. But anyway, she had jumped.

Well, now, she thought. This going up the face of East Rock was not in the same category as that time of being up on the barn roof and being scared to jump. Because this time she was on land. Her hands and feet were on land and there was no soaring through the air involved. It is true the land was practically perpendicular. Still it was land and all she had to do was keep her hands and feet on it and soon she would be at the top.

Rachel looked up. It was certainly a long way to the top. She couldn't even see the top, only copper-colored rock with here and there a tough weed to grab hold of. But see! What a good climber she was. Her father would soon be taking her with him on his arduous bird trips. And this reminded her of the owl eyries she hoped to see. She paused a moment and looked around. There were no owl eyries above her, or beside her, and — oh, here she made her big mistake — looking down, she saw none below her.

She saw no owl eyries below her but she did see what a high place she was on now, sticking like a fly to the side of a mountain. And suddenly, just like that time on the roof, she was afraid to keep on doing what she had been doing so very nicely. She was afraid to keep on going up.

The perpendicular swimmer, with his fondness

for the up-and-down position, might enjoy this, but not she. Furthermore, she did not see how, unless she slid, she was ever going to get back down. And there was Sam Doody to consider. He had to take pictures and here she was, holding up the works. Sam Doody or no Sam Doody, she could not go on. Rachel was clinging to a rather good spot, with hands and knees and toes, and she thought, *In a minute I will be able to go on, just as that time on the roof. When I finally did jump, it was as though I never had had the frightened time when I couldn't.*

So when her brother and Sam Doody called down to her, for they had kept right on up, never dreaming she was not at their heels, "Coming, Rachel?" she answered, "Soon. In a minute." She trusted the minute would not stretch into hours as that time on the roof.

Jerry kept right on climbing. But Sam Doody stopped and he looked down at Rachel.

"You OK?" he asked her.

"Sure," she said. But she could not budge.

In spite of her precarious position, Rachel's heart swelled with love for Sam Doody. She loved him next to her mother and father and Jerry and Uncle Bennie and Gramp and Gramma. He would bring her a sandwich if she stuck for always. Better still, he might not let her stick for always. This thought gave her great courage and she inched up another notch. But then she inched back because the new spot was not as good a spot to be stuck in as the old spot.

Then it dawned on Jerry, quite a few feet above, that his sister had stalled. Had he or Sam Doody, unwittingly, made some remark to Rachel that would scare her? A remark, for instance, such as he had once made to her when he and she were in swimming down at Sandy Beach? He had happened to mention that there were eels in the water and she got so scared he thought it was funny and added there were also sea monsters.

Then she had swum to the raft like sixty, screaming and gasping that there was an eel on her left shoulder. She was shuddering so she would not look to make sure, but she was positive it was, or at least had been, there. Probably she had swum into a long slithery piece of seaweed but she was convinced it was an eel. And she wouldn't swim back to shore no matter how much he told her he was joking and that an eel wouldn't hurt anyway and the monsters were a myth.

She wouldn't believe him and sat in the broiling sun on the raft, her arms folded around her knees, her eyes fastened dreamily on the shining water, and she wouldn't swim back, and she wouldn't swim back. Of course Jerry couldn't go home without her and he kept calling her and calling her. It was only after all the kids had gone home and the tide was low and there was not much water left to swim in, that she silently and calmly made her way back to land.

Well, he hadn't made any remarks now about monsters, and he doubted that Sam Doody had either. Anyway, what sort of monsters could cling to this precipice? But he, Jerry, never made a scary remark to Rachel at all anymore, because she believed everything, everything.

"What's the matter, Rachel?" he called down to her.

"It's so far to down."

"Don't look down."

"I already did."

"Must only look up."

"I saw down."

And there she stuck. There was nothing for Jerry and Sam Doody to do then but inch their way back down. Once they were past and below her, Jerry beside her and Sam below, Rachel was able to lower herself slowly back down the cliff. The going down took almost no time at all.

When Rachel looked back up she marveled at how little a way up they had gone. It had seemed a mile, at least, at the time. She was glad to be down on the ground again, flat ground, and she was very grateful that neither Jerry nor Sam Doody made any comments that she had altered the plans for the scaling of East Rock.

Sam Doody smiled his white-teeth smile just as always; and he gave her a piece of chocolate and off they went around the Rock to find the Giant Steps, which were the regular way up. And then Rachel found that Sam Doody never expected to reach top anyway. He said he wasn't going to let them go very far up. Too dangerous. He said, "There were a few kids tried to climb East Rock once and they had to call out the Fire Department to get them down."

"I was almost to the top," said Jerry proudly.

"Sure. Looked that way, anyway. And anyway we didn't have to call the Fire Department, did we? No," said Sam, answering his own question, a way he had of doing. He'd say, "Nice day, isn't it?" And then, because he was always in a hurry, he'd answer for you. "Fine," he'd say and stride on up the street with those long legs of his.

They halfway circled East Rock and then they started up the pleasant, gradual, green-wooded slope.

About halfway up there was rock again, not as sheer as the face had been and different colored—dark. And then, there at last, were the Giant Steps!

The Giant Steps were not exactly as Rachel had imagined they were going to be. She had thought they were going to be one enormous flight of huge stairs, made of marble most likely, leading straight up as far and high as you could see. These Giant Steps, however, were tremendous boulders that formed natural steps, though here and there other flat rocks had been pushed into place by man. Railings, also, had been built at the most dangerous twists and turnings. The steps were very exciting and Rachel clambered right up them like a mountain goat and she was not frightened at all. They were wonderful steps.

When they reached the top they were on a lovely greensward in the middle of which was a high monument. Tall Sam Doody took some pictures of it and also of a cannon that was there. He even took one picture of Jerry sitting on top of the cannon and one of Rachel standing at the base of the monument. Then they all admired the breathtaking view of the city. They could see the water, bluer than the sky, sparkling in the distance and, across the water, they could see Cranbury.

"I see the church on the Green," screamed Rachel excitedly. "Imagine seeing that far!"

"I see Long Island!" yelled Jerry.

After this they strolled down the other side of the Rock until they came to the little zoo, and they saw the bear and the raccoons. They also saw the gnu. But since they did not know how to pronounce this they called it the G N U. Sam Doody took some more pictures here. One of these should win, perhaps the one of the G N U.

By this time it was getting late and they were tired. They returned to the top of the Rock again and then down the Giant Steps, and finally, there they were, back at Sam Doody's jalopy again. Jerry had to rush back for his rocks he had almost forgotten and then off they went.

Sam Doody rode his jalopy with great style, one long leg flung carelessly over the door and dangling outside. And in great style he drove up to a corner drugstore and he treated all of them to a fifteen-cent ice cream soda. All together this cost him forty-five cents. Rachel and Jerry appreciated this further generosity on Sam Doody's part, for it would take dusting one half of the pews to earn that much money, and they knew how hard that was.

Sam dismissed their thanks with his good-natured shrug and grinned. "It's nothing," he assured them. He had got some very good pictures, he thought, and he hoped to get first prize with one of them. First prize was fifteen dollars. But if he did not get that, he hoped at least to get honorable mention which brought in fame but no money. Sort of on the order of Mr. Pye, reflected Rachel dreamily and listening lovingly to the loud breathing Sam Doody was doing through his mouth. It had been a comforting sound to hear, up on the high Rock.

"No sign of Ginger yet?" asked Sam Doody.

Jerry shook his head. Suddenly he remembered the beautiful eyes of Ginger pup, and his soft ears, and the funny sideways walk he had, and he gulped and looked down at his empty soda glass.

Once Jerry had explored East Rock he could see that it was not a place where he could expect to find Ginger. But he had kept his eyes and ears open anyway. Besides, he just had to explore everywhere for Ginger. He might crop up in the most unlikely place. Now, if someone would take them up West Rock someday soon, they would have been everywhere, he thought.

11

Judges Cave

Usually when the whole Pye family went on a picnic they went up Shingle Hill, or, if the picnic were to be a really long day's outing with a trolley ride involved first, they went up the Sleeping Giant. To-day, however, the Pyes were going up West Rock where they had never been before.

West Rock was the twin of East Rock, on the other side of the city. West Rock did not have Giant Steps going up it, nor did it have a monument, but somewhere on top it had a famous cave known as Judges Cave. The Cave was in history. After the three judges, Whalley, Dixwell, and Goffe had condemned Charles the First to be beheaded, they had escaped to this country and two of them, Colonel Whalley and Colonel Goffe, had hidden from the king's soldiers for three years in this cave on the top of West Rock. So the cave was known now as Judges Cave.

Both Jerry and Rachel knew plenty about caves from reading *Tom Sawyer* and pirate books. They knew what to expect from caves. To have sheltered the regicides for three years Judges Cave must be the greatest cave of all, they thought.

Jerry had an idea that Ginger might be located up there in Judges Cave. If, for instance, Ginger had been stolen by a band of counterfeiters, this band might be hiding, with Ginger as a watchdog, in Judges Cave. The more Jerry thought about this possibility the more excited he became. Last night, in the funny paper he had drawn for Rachel—sometimes, instead of both of them working on the same funny paper and their hands getting in each other's way, he drew one for her and she drew one for him—he had shown the yellow-hat band of counterfeiters lurking at the entrance of the great cave with him and Dick and Duke stealing up for a surprise attack and Ginger pup cooperating by not barking and giving them away, hardly able to keep from wagging his tail, though he was so happy to smell freedom near.

To think that all the while Jerry and Rachel had been searching Cranbury for Ginger he might have been being held captive by the band of counterfeiters in the cave on West Rock. That was what Jerry was thinking as he drew his funny paper. Had either he or Rachel ever seen Judges Cave, he would have realized how impossible this would be. However, neither he nor she had. Today they were going to see it though, at least so they thought.

On this expedition Mr. Pye, and not Sam Doody, was going to be the leader. It was quite a party—Mr. and Mrs. Pye, Jerry, Rachel, Uncle Bennie, Gramma (not Grampa, he had to tune the church organ), Dick Badger, and Duke. If Ginger had been there, then the family would have been complete, except of course for Grampa and for Gracie-the-cat who preferred sleep to seeing the world anyway.

When Ginger had been there, Gracie-the-cat had acted like a young kitten again, romping with him, and enjoying the attention he gave her of biting her fleas for her, going over her with his sharp little teeth from head to toe several times a day. This was most refreshing to Gracie. But since the disappearance of Ginger Pye, Gracie did practically nothing but sleep. She frequently stayed in nights now. She snoozed, day in, day out. She did not mind in the least when all the Pyes went off for Judges Cave, leaving her all by herself in the high house.

The trolley car that the Pyes took was practically empty and this was lucky since they were such a big party, what with lunch baskets, blankets, Duke, and all. The little old motorman did not like the idea of Duke being on his trolley. He didn't like any dog on his trolley, but a huge one on the order of Duke was worst of all.

Mr. Pye said persuasively to the motorman, "Well, of course, if this was the rush hour, we would not be doing such a thing. But since it is not the rush hour, what does it matter?"

So the motorman said all right and then he clamped his tight little jaws together, he was so disapproving. Then he said that, rush hour or not, someone must stand in the rear of the trolley and keep the big hound dog there.

This pleased Dick anyway for it is more interesting on a trolley to stand, either in the front or
the back, than to sit. Of course Jerry stood back
there with Dick and Duke. But Rachel, happy at
the idea of going on a cave-and-bird trip with Papa,
sat between him and Uncle Bennie, whenever Uncle
Bennie was sitting, that is. A great deal of the time
Uncle Bennie was racing back and forth and up and

down the trolley. The conductor said he was worse than Duke.

"He does not nip or bite," said Papa. And he said that Uncle Bennie was hardly disturbing anyone since there was only one other passenger besides the Pyes on this trolley, at present anyway.

This other passenger was a Mr. Tuttle, the tall short man who, sitting in his pew in church, looked as tall as Judge Ball and Sam Doody, but who, the minute he stood up, was shorter than Papa, who was of medium height. Now, on the trolley, this Mr. Tuttle was lost in thought, his hands cupped on his chin, his face plastered to the window. He did not even change his thoughtful expression when Uncle Bennie careened merrily against his knees.

Everyone in Cranbury knew Mr. Tuttle. With silent wags of the head and a few words formed silently with their lips, all the Pye picnickers agreed that Mr. Tuttle's present pose, that of being lost in thought, was a most unusual one for him. Ordinarily, he had an expression best described as "alerted."

Mr. Tuttle was just the opposite of the unsavory character, for Mr. Tuttle was a doer of good deeds. Watching him now, Rachel thought of some of the good deeds she knew of that he had done and was famous for. Once, during the Christmas pageant in church, the wings of one of the little angels caught on fire from a candle. Mr. Tuttle saw this before anyone else was even aware of the danger. He rushed up the aisle, though this was church and a solemn festival was going on, and he flung his overcoat over the little angel, putting the fire out with no harm done at all except for a singed wing. Quick thinking of this sort was what this good character was noted for.

On trolleys, even when they were empty and he could choose from plenty of good places to sit, Mr. Tuttle never sat down at all. He always stood at the back of the trolley watching that boys did not jump on the cow fender and hurt themselves. Also, from his regular spot in the rear, he could open the window, reach out and adjust the trolley if it came off the wire, so that the tired motorman would not have to get up and do this. He also knew where all the switches along the route were that might have to be changed. At these points he was right up front then, waiting to get out the front door, switch stick in hand, to make the adjustment. He did this, getting from the back to the front of the car, with no fuss at all or pushing people aside. It was as though he floated through the air to the spot where he was most needed.

These were the reasons why it was so surprising to the Pyes that he was sitting now in an ordinary seat. The Pyes thought it was a wonder that the Second Avenue trolley line did not put him on the payroll. But he would not have liked this for he did things out of the kindness of his heart and for no other reason.

Now, suddenly, the tall short man stood up. He raced to the front of the car and ordered the motorman to stop. No one would dream of disobeying Mr. Tuttle, even a motorman, and he stopped the car. All the Pyes waited curiously for developments, imagining Mr. Tuttle had seen a dog fight, perhaps, and was bent on separating the dogs.

But that was not it. Mr. Tuttle's face wore an expression of suppressed excitement as, presently, he thrust it back into the trolley.

"Clear the trolley," he ordered.

The motorman was inclined to demur for he was acquainted only with Mr. Tuttle's switch and trolley activities. He knew nothing of the angel in church and fires.

"The trolley happens to be on fire," said the tall short man.

The motorman grumpily turned around and gave a general get-out gesture to the Pyes.

"Women and children first," said Mr. Tuttle gallantly.

All the Pyes filed out. Duke seemed very pleased. Mr. Tuttle shepherded them in the proper order as though saving them from the *Titanic*. All looked under the trolley and, sure enough, a little smoke thinly wafted its way out.

"We could make it to the car barn," grumbled the motorman.

"Not with women and children aboard," sternly rebuked the tall short man.

This was all a great nuisance, for the Pyes with all their paraphernalia had to wait for the next trolley. When it came along it had to go very slowly because the simmering one they had just evacuated preceded them and could not go fast. At this rate would they ever get to West Rock? Mr. Tuttle stayed with the motorman on the burning car, so at least there were no more stops and catastrophes.

But that incident showed the kind of a man Mr. Tuttle was. Unexpected. There he had been, sitting, and giving the impression he was not on the alert at all, whereas, actually, underneath the quiet exterior, he had probably been sniffing and smelling, all his senses on the alert for the right moment to make the rescue.

Rachel could not help thinking that if there were anyone whom they should ask to help them find Ginger, that man was Mr. Tuttle. Why had they not thought of it sooner? Next time she saw him she would bring the matter up. But here, at last, they had reached West Rock, and once more the Pyes piled out.

The face of West Rock was even sheerer and higher than that of East Rock. Thank goodness, thought Rachel, nothing was said about climbing *it*. Papa carried Uncle Bennie pickaback most of the way up. They had to climb West Rock at its least steep part, therefore. Uncle Bennie had wanted to go up it on Duke's back, but this was not permitted. However, he enjoyed the ride on Papa almost as much.

While Mama and Gramma were spreading the picnic on a big flat rock, Rachel, and Jerry, and Uncle Bennie, and Dick, with Duke loping along in fine spirits, went on a preliminary exploring expedition to find Judges Cave. The regicides had hidden in it for three years so it must be a very fine cave. In it they might find not only Ginger amidst the counterfeiters, but also Indian arrowheads and bits of flint, perhaps even a real live Indian forgotten here through the years.

Up here the Indians seemed so real to Rachel she almost expected to see them posed, statuelike, behind every tree. Whenever she went walking through thick woods she had the feeling that Indians still lived there, that she would see them stealing from tree to tree. It was because in school they read and studied so much about the Indians that it seemed they must still be there, lurking in the woods.

They saw no Indians. But the woods they walked through were thick and beautiful. Squirrels were refurnishing their nests, buds were coming out, dogwood was in bloom, and the forsythia was a brilliant sheath of gold. Mountain laurel, also, was in bloom.

Uncle Bennie filled his pockets with little acorns and pinecones, Jerry found some fine chunks of rock, Rachel kept her eyes open for an interesting bird story to report to Papa, and Dick whittled on a piece of hickory. All kept their eyes out for the cave, hoping to be the discoverer.

Suddenly Uncle Bennie said, "Oh-h-h."

He sounded so ecstatic the others all thought of course he had sighted the cave. This was not so. But he had found a little robin's egg, all whole, that had fallen out of a nest. It had landed on a soft bed of moss and Uncle Bennie lovingly picked it up. He held it in the palm of his hand, transfixed with delight.

"My little Easter egg," he murmured.

On Easter, he and Rachel and Jerry had hunted all over the house for all the regular big painted eggs the Bunny had hidden. Now, here was this little Easter egg, just his size, hidden way up here on West Rock. Who would have expected such a surprise?

The others were as pleased as he was. "Hold it carefully," they said. "Take it home, and maybe a little robin will hatch out."

For a while Uncle Bennie held the little blue egg very carefully. He could hardly walk he held it so carefully. But then, being hungry and recalling how delicious Easter eggs are, he took a little bite. He had imagined this special little egg, just his size, would taste even better than regular ones. Nothing could have been further from his expectations than the way it really did taste.

"Ugh!" exclaimed Uncle Bennie, spitting it out and sputtering "Mouth, mouth," as he always did when something unpleasant got in his mouth.

"Uncle Bennie," reproved the others. "That wasn't a egg to eat. That was a little egg to hatch a little robin out of."

For a time it looked as though Uncle Bennie, though he was not a whiner, was going to cry. Rachel wiped his mouth out on her dress. He moaned, "My little Easter egg. Gaw gone."

"Maybe you will find another one," suggested Rachel, to console him.

Uncle Bennie shook his head. "My little tiny Easter egg," he said. "Not good to eat." His disappointment was very great.

The others told him he was soon to see a big cave and after a while Uncle Bennie forgot his little egg. Rachel put the broken shell in her pocket to show Papa. So far, the robin's egg was the most interesting part of the picnic, for when they heard Papa whistling for them to come to lunch they had still seen no sign of the cave.

"We'll find it after lunch," Jerry assured them. "Naturally an important cave is not easy to find, or it would not be an important cave." The harder the cave was to find, Jerry reasoned, the more likely it was to be a hideaway for counterfeiters, and hence, the more likely a place for Ginger to have been kept.

When the children got back to the grown-ups, there the picnic was, all spread out on a khaki-colored old army blanket. They had sandwiches, hard eggs, bananas, dill pickles, potato salad, baked beans, baked ham, jelly doughnuts, and homemade chocolate cake. After eating as much as they possibly could Gramma said, "Now, take a little nap."

Naturally the children did not want to take a little nap and miss all of life.

Mama agreed with Gramma that they should rest awhile after such a monumental meal before going cave hunting again. But the children assured her cave hunting was not in the same category as swimming when, of course, they knew they must rest an hour before going in the water. In cave hunting, they told their mother, there is no danger of cramps.

Since they weren't resting anyway, just jumping around being wild Indians and climbing trees, Mama said, "All right. Go off and find the cave. But be sure to come back when you hear Papa whistle."

"Yes," the children yelled and off they ran, this time without Uncle Bennie who, the minute he saw old Bubbah, had, after all, fallen asleep. There he lay in the warm sunshine with old Bubbah wound around him and traces of jelly doughnut on his moist lips.

Now that their stomachs were full, the children were bounding with energy. They had lots of time, they could go far, they would really find the cave. The cave! Thinking about the cave, and not having found it yet, the cave had taken on fabulous proportions in their minds. They bet there was an underground spring in it even, maybe, or a lost river.

They zigzagged back and forth through the woods and across the green grass. In the distance they saw an iron fence surrounding some huge boulders so they went to examine this. On the fence was a sign. "Judges Cave," said the sign and gave a short history of the regicides. The children looked at Judges Cave incredulously.

"This is not the *real* cave, is it?" asked Rachel.

"Can't be," said Jerry.

"Must be," said Dick. "Sign says so."

What a cave! Iron fencing all around it, a sign saying to keep out, even barbed wire along the top of the fence. They couldn't see the entrance to the cave. They couldn't tell how deep into the earth and rock it went. They couldn't tell whether this cave was like the cave in *Tom Sawyer* or what it was like.

"Why do they keep it fenced off?" asked Jerry. "What a cave it must be! Wouldn't you think they'd let you in?"

"Let's go in anyway," suggested Dick Badger.

"How? With the wire and all? And it's against the law, it says," demurred Rachel. "It says so in plain English. Keep out."

"What's the use of a cave if you can't get in it?" they all grumbled.

They sat down a moment and studied whether

they could see in the cave anywhere at all. They crawled around on their stomachs for better views. No one could possibly realize that inside these great and broken rocks and boulders a wonderful cave was hidden. There the boulders sat on the green grass, in the middle of their private little fenced-off place. No wonder the regicides had been able to hide for three years in a cave like this that didn't look like a cave at all; it looked only like any great chunks of boulder inside a cage. Naturally the cage part had not been here when the regicides hid in the cave. The iron railing was a modern invention.

"In old times, it was better," said Rachel. "They did not have cages around things."

"Still, this is a perfect place for counterfeiters and dog thieves to hide," reflected Jerry. He was reluctant to give up the idea of the counterfeiters. "Detectives would never think to look for them in there with all the signs and the wire and fence to keep out."

The children thought excitedly of the forbidden cave. Recovering from their first disappointment they began to think the cave must, indeed, be a very special one to be fenced off like this. If they could only have one peek in it, just one little crawl.

They sat on the grass considering the cave so

long Rachel almost thought, in the deepening shadows of afternoon, that she could see a regicide stick his head out of the very ground for a second and then disappear. Oh, to get inside the cave! To be this near a real cave and not to be able to get into it! What was the use of the cave? That was what they wondered disconsolately. But they could not break a law that was printed in plain English right before their very eyes.

"Never say die" was the motto of Dick Badger. "It doesn't say, 'No dogs allowed,' and we could boost Duke over," he said. "We could tie a long string to him and, unwinding it, we could tell how far in he goes, say a hundred yards, or a mile, or what."

"I have a long string, but not a mile of string," said Jerry.

Unfortunately, in the end they all had to ruefully admit that even sending Duke in was impossible, what with the iron fencing and the barbed wire too. The men who put up this fence really meant it when they said stay out. They meant dogs too, without a doubt.

There was one other possibility. Maybe this cave had another entrance or exit hidden nearby. They hunted around in the woods and they commanded

Duke to do likewise and find more cave. Duke obligingly sniffed around but he did not disappear anywhere nor sink into the earth, in spite of their earnest entreaties. He wanted to loll on the sunny sward, that was all.

The search for the other entrance which they were not sure existed anyway occupied them until they heard Mr. Pye's whistle and they had to go back. The children complained to Mr. Pye about the cave and he said the whole party would go back that way and at least see the outside of the historic site about which many authors, including Scott and Cooper, had written stories.

"See, Papa," said Jerry wearily, when once more they stood outside the cave of the regicides. "It says, 'Keep out.' Why?"

"Of course," said Mr. Pye. "I could have told you that. It is to keep souvenir hunters from chipping it all away."

"Mean to say souvenir hunters would take away Judges Cave?" asked Rachel. "How could they take away a cave, which is a hole?"

"They chip away a piece here, and a piece there, and soon you have no cave. There are fences around most historic sites so souvenir hunters won't swipe the entire business. Around Plymouth Rock, for instance. There's a fence around it, and other such places."

"Oh," said the children, glad there was some sensible explanation to fences.

But imagine people chipping away things! What was the matter with people, anyway, that was what they wanted to know. If people didn't go around chipping pieces off caves and rocks and things they could have got into the cave and played pirate and explored it and had a wonderful time.

But then Papa said, so they would not be too disappointed, that he had heard that Judges Cave had caved in anyway. So even if there had not been a fence around it they probably would not have seen much. The great cave was probably no longer really a cave after all. It was lucky the regicides hid when they had or they probably would have had to find a different place to escape from the king's soldiers than this.

Tiredly, they trudged the long way down the Rock to the street where the trolley ran. They did not have to wait long for their trolley and this motorman did not seem to mind a big dog like Duke boarding his car. He made no comments at all. This was a more modern trolley than the one they had come out in, and Jerry and Dick sat together in one side seat with Duke on the floor at their feet, his tail in the aisle. Papa and Rachel sat opposite them. They had turned their seat back so they could face Mama and Gramma, who had Uncle Bennie on her lap. In this way they could all talk to one another without turning their heads and getting a crick in their necks. They were all very weary and even Uncle Bennie was content to sit on the return trip and not go careening.

Jerry was especially tired and, moreover, he did not feel good. Maybe it was because he was so tired, or because he did not feel good, and because here it was springtime and Ginger had been stolen so long ago, at the beginning of winter. Anyway, for the first time, Jerry began to despair of ever finding his dog.

He didn't tell Dick or Rachel that hope was waning, because he didn't think they knew that he was still searching for Ginger. They didn't know that everywhere he went—up East Rock, up West Rock, all over everywhere, he kept his eyes open for some clue as to Ginger's whereabouts. But he did. And now, where could he look? he asked himself sadly.

Rachel saw how sad Jerry looked. He is thinking about Ginger, she decided and she felt sad herself. She knew that Judges Cave was sort of Jerry's last hope. She and Jerry rarely talked of finding Ginger anymore. When they spoke of him they only always said, "Remember how Ginger used to do this, or do that? Remember?" they would ask fondly.

Rachel wished now that she could think of some way to help Jerry keep on hoping. She still hoped and he should too. It seemed to Rachel that they had to go on searching for Ginger and never give up searching. They had, at least, to find out what had happened to him. And then Rachel said a silent little prayer. *Help me to help Jerry find Ginger,* she prayed. And then—could it be in answer to her prayer?—the tall short man, Mr. Tuttle, the doer of good deeds, got on their trolley at the corner of Church and Chapel. Wasn't it odd that he should get on their same trolley both going and coming? Rachel believed in signs and omens and she again had the notion, just as this morning, that this good man might be of help in locating Ginger Pye.

She sat there, trembling with excitement because she was going to do such a daring thing as branch out all by herself and solicit the help of this man who, though she knew him, certainly did not know her. At any rate he never said hello or good-bye.

She studied the man in admiration. She thought of his brave deeds. There he had sat, this morning, this doer of good deeds, quietly and not looking alerted, until all of a sudden he had ordered the trolley stopped and had made the passengers pile out, un-panicstricken. The minute he had got on the trolley he had probably taken a good sniff and he had probably smelled that something was wrong. And he had just sat there sniffing and smelling until he had figured out what. And then he had sprung into action.

How would he be about finding dogs? Rachel wondered. Just fine, she answered herself, the way Sam Doody did.

Of course she could not ask him this second with all the family around. When the family got off the trolley she would find some way of staying on for just a few more blocks and she would talk then to the doer of good deeds. She could not take her eyes off him.

It was a wonderful ride home. Mr. Tuttle stood alerted in his regular spot at the rear of the trolley. But no children jumped on the cow fender. The trolley did not come off the wire, and there was no little smolder or smoke. Furthermore, all the switches seemed to be adjusted and of course there were no Christmas angels around.

This was all a great relief to the tired Pyes who wanted only to get home, now the long day's picnic had ended, and who had groaned slightly at the sight of Mr. Tuttle, not knowing he was in answer to

Rachel's prayer. At the Pyes' corner they all filed off and did not seem to notice that Rachel stayed on. She watched them straggle up the street, dropping blankets and bags and gathering them up, and she laughed to herself thinking how they had not missed her and doubtless imagined she was bringing up the rear.

Now was the time to speak to the alert Mr. Tuttle before the trolley reached his corner. Yes, now was the perfect time to ask the good man's help. With her heart pounding a little she went down the aisle and stood beside him. How to begin? He was sitting on the motorman's little stool, and looked tall.

"Mister," said Rachel.

Mr. Tuttle did not bend his head. He doubtless was studying the scene outside for potential catastrophes.

"Oh, Mr. Tuttle," said Rachel.

The tall short man, and sitting down he was awfully tall, turned his faraway gaze down upon Rachel.

"Are you lost, child?" he asked benignly.

"No, I'm not. My dog is," said Rachel, barging right in.

"Your dog got off at Beam's Place along with the rest of your family."

"That's not my dog."

"Well, if he is a lost dog, he must be turned over to the police. They will endeavor to locate his true owner."

For a moment Rachel was bewildered. Then she said, lurching a bit as the trolley turned a corner, "The dog you saw with us was Dick's dog, not our dog. Dick's dog is not a lost dog. Ours is."

So then this Mr. Tuttle said very wisely, "Your dog is lost, so is not found. But when he's found he'll not be lost."

And then this tall short man stood up. He commanded the motorman to stop. He told the motorman to wait for him. He took Rachel by the hand, helped her off the trolley, stopped the trolley coming the other way, put her on it, told the motorman to let her off at Beam's Place—no fare required, no questions asked—got back on his trolley, and off it went with him, and off Rachel's went with her.

When Rachel recovered from the surprise she said to herself, "That man is more interested in sudden perils than in past ones." Nothing had been gained by staying on the trolley and trying to tell him the story of lost Ginger. But then, nothing had been lost.

She repeated to herself wonderingly, "Your dog is lost so is not found. But when he's found, he'll not be lost." As she got off the trolley and ran home she could not help laughing. It did sound so funny. She bet that would make Jerry laugh. She bet it would.

12

Tramps and the Sunny Fields

When Rachel reached home after her unsuccessful encounter with the tall short man she found that she had not been missed. She also found that it was not a good time to tell Jerry what the tall short man had said because Jerry had been put to bed.

"Stick out your tongue," Mama had said to him the minute they got in the house and she had immediately suspected that he had the German measles. Uncle Bennie had been hurried home in the hope that he would not catch them too, and Rachel was permitted to speak to him only from the distance. The nearest she could come to him was her doorway, though she had had real measles once and the German variety a couple of times.

Mama telephoned Dr. Kelly, and Rachel and Jerry made guesses as to whether he would bring the pink or the green medicine. Both tasted awful but the green was worse since it also looked bad.

Meanwhile Mama got out a little bottle of Dr. Bing's sugar pills.

There were Dr. Bing pills for all ills. They came in a sweet little bottle with a number on it. All you had to do was select the right number from a little book and give the pills and wait for the cure. Last time that Rachel had had German measles she made such a rapid recovery Mama said, "My. These pills are truly remarkable." Then when Rachel got well and Mama was giving her room a good airing and cleaning out, what did she find but dozens and dozens of the remarkable pills lined up along the baseboard behind the bed. That was what Rachel had done to them instead of swallowing them, she had dropped them behind the bed, for she was suspicious of all pills.

Naturally, since Rachel had got well without them, Mama no longer had quite the faith in the little sugar pills that she used to. But until Dr. Kelly got there with the pink or the green, she felt she was doing something to make Jerry well, giving him the six little pellets. Jerry liked them very well and did not drop them behind the bed.

Jerry was very disgusted to think he would have to spend, perhaps, a whole week in bed. He didn't feel *that* sick, he said. But he did have to and Rachel racked her brains to think of things to make him happy, especially when it proved to be the green medicine he had to take.

As Jerry lay in bed looking out the window at the huge horse chestnut tree beginning to blossom, he didn't know why but he kept thinking about an old brick lot over on New Dollar Street. This lot was called the brick lot because it was chuck-full of old broken bricks from an old manor house that had once stood over there and had burned down. In this lot there were two huge rocks that were supposed to be meteors. Jerry had heard they were cutting a new street behind that lot. And the thought kept occurring to him that since Ginger, after all, was not to be found in such far and hard places as East Rock or West Rock, he might possibly be hidden in some new house in the new street in back of the houses on New Dollar Street.

He and Rachel had searched on New Dollar Street itself. But they had not investigated the old brick lot, nor the fields behind, nor the place where the new street was being cut.

"Rache," Jerry called out one evening. "What happens to the little brooks when towns grow up, new houses are built, and streets. Where do the little brooks go?"

This was a stumper, this question was, and Rachel did not know.

And Jerry fell to thinking about Ginger again. "Rachel," he said. He had just a little fever and it was at night, when the fever was highest, that he did most of his talking. "Rachel," he said. "Do you think the meteors are still over in the old brick lot?" He didn't bring up about Ginger, he just brought up about the meteors.

Rachel said, "Of course they are. Who could take such big things?"

Jerry said, "The Cranbury Historical Society. I should think they would want such valuable pieces of rock. They're not rock, they're meteors. They are most as big as the ones down at the Museum of Natural History in New York. I wouldn't mind having them here in the backyard to study."

"The Moffats may have got them for their museum."

The Moffats were a family over near Ashbellows Place who had a museum in their barn, "The Moffats' Museum."

"They might have," agreed Jerry. "You must see."

"To be a rock man must you study not only the rock of this earth but the rock of fallen stars too?" asked Rachel, impressed.

"Everything," said Jerry importantly.

"Well, I can't get them for you. They are too big for us even to get together. But I'll go and see if they are still there and tell you."

"Might take a little look around for Ginger over there," said Jerry, trying to sound offhand. "Might be a little house built over there in back of the maple groves that we hadn't heard of. And Ginger might of been there all the time, tied up, waiting for us to come and find him."

"I'll go tomorrow," promised Rachel, and Jerry went to sleep.

Before Rachel fell asleep she thought she might be a better finder of Ginger if she joined the Brownie Scouts as Addie Egan had been urging her to do for some time. She had not joined so far because of the Aurora Borealis. She had gone to one meeting of the Brownie Scouts one cold winter evening. When she came out she found people standing around gaping at the heavens, exclaiming over the glorious spectacle they had witnessed of the Aurora Borealis. It was about over. Rachel should have seen it a few minutes before, said Jerry.

So Rachel had not gone to any more meetings of the Brownie Scouts in case she miss the Aurora Borealis again. Still, now she thought—for she had to think of *something* before going to sleep now

that Martin Boombernickles was postponed indef-
initely—perhaps she would be a better finder of
Ginger if she joined up and learned lore of different
sorts. And she, too, went to sleep.

Rachel planned to go to the brick lot with Addie
Egan. But Addie also had the measles as she found
out the next afternoon when she whistled for her.
This made Rachel feel very lonesome and as though
she were the only one in the world without measles.
Mama saw how lonesome she felt and gave her two
pennies to spend, one for her and one for Jerry.

"What do you want?" Rachel called up the stairs
to Jerry.

"A yo-yo," said Jerry. "They have them in that
penny shop behind the fields, behind the old brick
lot."

"That's where I was going anyway," said Rachel.
Jerry needn't think she had forgotten about the meteors or anything. Now, she had so many purposes,
her head swam. One to look for Ginger in the fields
and new houses. Two, to examine the meteors, and
make sure they were still there. Three, to spend the
pennies. One, two, three. Supposing she should be
the one to find Ginger all by herself? And bring him
home to Jerry? And Jerry should suddenly get well
of the measles, the measles falling off him like little

pink sugar pellets? He would be so happy, and there would be him and her and Ginger again, as there used to be. And Gracie, too.

It was such a bright sparkling day anything might happen. She might pick some tall violets also by a little brook. Her head spun weaving these lovely plans and she ran all the way over to New Dollar Street. This was really quite a long run and she arrived at the old brick lot hot, panting, and out of breath.

The meteors were still there and she climbed up on one to rest and consider. These were truly wonderful big meteors, square chunks of red-purple

rock. It was astonishing to think that two pieces of star would break off in such neat, perfect rectangular-shaped blocks and land right here side by side in the old brick lot. It was lucky they had not landed on the yellow house next door, where once the Moffats had lived.

Some grown-ups had the idea these rocks were not meteors at all, but were parts of the foundation of the huge brick manor house that used to stand in this lot. But all the children knew better than that. They knew the rocks were meteors, parts of star, that had come shooting through the air and landed here. It was surprising a fence had not been put around the meteors, as around Judges Cave. Souvenir hunters might begin chipping them all away.

Rachel examined the meteors all over to see if she could find a little piece of mica for Jerry. She did find a tiny speck shining in the sun and she chipped this off and put it in her pocket for him. She didn't think she was in a class with souvenir hunters who would chip away the whole thing, for mica was something extra that was added, not the meteors themselves. It was Rachel's intention to bring home plenty of treasures to Jerry. She found an interesting rock and put it in her pocket, hoping it was quartz. She still didn't know whether a rock was a quartz or not. But then, she was not going to be a rock man; she was going to be a bird man and help Papa. She was already a member of the Audubon Bird Society and she always wore her button. She had it on now.

In the brick lot and beyond, in the broad sunny fields, a deceptive quiet prevailed. The quiet was of the sun and the sky. It was not a field quiet for crickets and grasshoppers were making a racket and jumping all over the place. Rachel sat on her meteor listening to the sounds of the insects and turning her two Indian pennies over and over in her moist palm.

Though it was only May it was as hot as the hot height of summer. The fields with their multitude of restless insects stretched far and wide. They were carpeted with tall field grass which later on would, she knew, reach above her waist. Sturdy field flowers, Indian pipe, star grass, and sour grass, with butter-and-eggs, daisies, and even buttercups beginning to blossom, made a varied pattern.

Rachel jumped off her meteor and wandered unevenly across the flashing sunny field that led eventually to the toy store. She would have liked to stop and gather an enormous bouquet for Mama, but gathering a big bouquet was not in the one, two, three errands she had for today.

Ordinarily when she and Jerry came over to this field, they picked such big bunches of flowers they could hardly hold on to them. They had to use both fists. They couldn't ever put the bouquets down on the ground. If they did, no matter how carefully they had laid them there, though at first they might stay in a fine firm bunch, suddenly they would sag and spread out like jackstraws and it was almost impossible to gather them up again.

She found the new street and the new houses being built, but the houses were still in the skeleton stage and there seemed no place where Ginger would be likely to be concealed, either in the fields or the new houses. So two of her errands were done—seeing that the meteors were still here, they were; seeing whether there was any sign of an imprisoned Ginger, there wasn't. Now she had only to cross another wide sunny field, go through a dense little thicket, cross a little brook, and she would come out on the street where the penny shop was.

As she sauntered along she listened to the sounds, the hot music of the insects, the low murmur of a small buckle shop in the distance. She hoped she would not hear the whistle. There was a strange sort of whistle that could be heard in this lot. It started low and worked itself up to a screaming high note in a series of gasps. It was a horrible sound. "What is it, do you suppose?" she once asked Addie Egan who happened to be with her, looking for things—empty cigarette boxes, tinfoil, red glass, and treasures in general. "It's the Gypsies at five o'clock," said Addie.

That was all Addie said and she said it in so positive a manner that Rachel would not have dreamed of asking for more information. "Oh, of course," said Rachel. After all, she had been wrong and Addie had been right about vilyun being villun. Rachel decided the whistle was a signal for all the Gypsies all over the world to get together around the campfire for their pot of stew. Possibly they gathered in this lot in the maple grove. One thing Rachel did not want was to be in this field all by herself at five o'clock for the stew gathering, though the spectacle would be interesting.

Then, suddenly, Rachel began to think about all the tramps. And suddenly, the sun having gone under a cloud, instead of the familiar fields of daytime in which she played and picked flowers, the fields had become the perilous fields of nighttime. It would have pleased Rachel simply to go back home, or at least go back to the main streets and get to the penny shop the safe and other way. However, she had come this far, the whistle had not blown, it was not five o'clock, it was not nighttime, the sun had come out from under the cloud, what was the sense of going back?

When she and Jerry and, sometimes, Uncle Bennie sat on their little upper veranda at home on Beam's Place, and looked across the street to their own field, watching twilight inch across it, every man they saw there was a terrible tramp. A terrible tramp with his sacks and burlap bags. But, Rachel reassured herself now, plucking a piece of sour grass and chewing it, these were not the evening fields of tramps and burlap bags, these were the sunny fields of daytime. Moreover, all tramps are not bad, she reminded herself happily as she trudged across the field.

When a tramp knocked at the back door Mama always gave him a bowl of soup, a cup of coffee and a bun, or whatever she happened to have on hand, even apple pie. These tramps usually came in the morning when Rachel and Jerry were at school. However, once one came on a Saturday morning and Mama gave this tramp a plate of steaming corn beef and cabbage. "My, he went for that!" said Mama happily, for Mama, like Gramma, loved to see people eat. "He cleaned the plate," she said with satisfaction.

Mama said the tramps had her door marked, so many of them came and asked for a cup of coffee. Rachel was familiar with marks on doors from reading *The Tinder Box*. She often studied their back door for this secret mark the tramps had placed there but she could not find it.

"Oh, it's invisible," her mother said. "The tramps have a secret way of passing the news on to one another as to who has a kind heart and will give them a bite and not sick the dog on them. It goes way back in my family," she said, "never to turn a hungry person away from the door."

"Do the tramps have Gramma marked too?" asked Rachel.

"Gramma, too," said Mama. And she would then tell the story about the poor old fellow in New York, not that he had come to their door exactly.

It happened that one night when Mama and her family were living for a time right in the heart of New York City, they had an extra pork chop for dinner. No one wanted it. Everyone had had enough to eat. The chop was brown and crisp and fresh and it was a pity not to have it eaten up immediately while it was so good. That was what they thought.

So Mama—this all happened just a few years before she met Papa on the escalator—put the chop on a clean paper napkin and carried it downstairs and laid it carefully on the top of the ash can. "They pick up your ashes and garbage every day in New York," Mama explained. "You have these big cans to put your rubbish in and by morning, presto, your rubbish has been removed. Not like this town where you have to pay for everything."

Then Mama had gone back upstairs and she and her Mama, that is Gramma, had watched from the window. Presently along there came a poor old man. Did he brighten up when he saw this beautiful chop! And he didn't have to go rummaging through the garbage for it either. There it lay, nice and clean and still warm, mind you, right on top of the ashes. Even so, he thought there must be a catch to it and he took it to the lamplight and examined every inch of it and sniffed it. It smelled so good and then, did he eat it!

Every time Rachel ate a pork chop she thought about the one the poor old fellow had had that he hadn't had to rummage through the garbage for, and she wondered if hers tasted as good. It seemed to her that his was the best pork chop there ever was, the way it was told.

Those tramps, the ones who came to the back door for a cup of coffee and the pork-chop tramp,

happened to be good ones. But there were bad ones too, her pounding heart reminded her as she entered the dark woods, leaving the sunny fields behind.

The woods were hushed, but already she could hear the tinkling music of the swift and clear little brook at the end of them. After the sunshine it seemed very dark in the woods but Rachel did not run because running, she cautioned herself, makes you scared. And she picked her way quickly over the roots and rocks that covered the path.

But then, had thinking about tramps made a tramp appear? Just as thinking about shooting stars sometimes made a shooting star appear, or a four leaf clover in a patch of threes? Anyway, there was a tramp lying under a tree on the side of the path, halfway in the thick bushes, his hat over his eyes.

Rachel stopped short. Was he asleep? She moved on quickly but softly, hoping he was really asleep and not merely pretending in order to grab her and put her in the burlap bag his head was resting on. She hoped, too, he was one of the good sort of tramp who knew about the mark on her back door and on Gramma's door, and how the marks went way back in her family, probably to Great-Gramma. And that here he was, this good sort of tramp, just taking a little nap.

As Rachel tiptoed past the sleeping tramp she tried not to think of the burlap-bag tramps about whom she and Jerry made up spooky stories. She tried to think only of the pork-chop tramp. Nevertheless her heart did pound and once she was well past him she broke into a wild run, leaping across the brook without stepping on the rock steps, and she did not stop running until she came out of the woods into the bright sunshine beside the little penny shop.

Then she thought, that tramp back there might not have been a good sort of tramp or a bad sort of tramp either. He might have been the mysterious footstepper, the unsavory character. Here she might have had a chance to get a clue about Ginger and what had she done? She had run. What color had this tramp's hat been? She had been too frightened to notice. She could tiptoe back and see what color the tramp's hat was, that was all. She could stand on the safe side of the brook, this side, and just look at his hat that was pulled down on his face so he could sleep.

At this moment, however, her tramp ambled out of the little side path. He didn't even look at her, but she looked at him. He didn't look at all like her and Jerry's villain, and she saw that his hat was black. It was not an old yellow one like Unsavory's at all. This was a great relief for, if it had been yellow, how would she ever have got to see whether or not it had the red mark inside the band that the perpendicular swimmer had put in the real hat?

Thank goodness, this tramp was very likely of the cup-of-coffee variety and not the sort who would steal Ginger. Anyway, Mama had said the person who stole Ginger was probably not a tramp at all but an unsavory character. So Rachel really could skip all tramps, if she saw any more of them, that is, on this particular day when it was her special job to search for Ginger, Jerry being sick with the measles.

Rachel went into Mrs. Tally's penny shop and after buying the yo-yo for Jerry she stood before the little glass showcase for a long long time. She was trying to make the impossible decision of choosing between a minature china doll with arms and legs that moved and long black hair, and a penny box of crayons. The lady of this shop did not care how long it took you to decide. At last Rachel bought the crayons and they became only a little soft and bent as she sauntered along the sunny streets home.

A man was leading his cow out of the fields that she had crossed a short time before. She was glad she had not seen the cow grazing then because she had on a red dress. Rachel had an idea that cows did not like red, though Jerry said it was bulls that did not like red, and that cows did not care what color you had on, and that she was mixed up. Even

so, what with the Gypsies at five o'clock, and the sleeping tramp, Rachel was glad she had not also seen the cow and had not had to think was it bulls or cows that did not like red.

The man and his cow loped placidly up the street ahead of Rachel. As she turned into her own street, leaving them loping along the main road, it seemed to Rachel she had been gone a very long time. She ran around to the back entrance way to see where Mama was, what everybody was doing.

Mama was giving some milk and some fish to a stray cat.

"Do cats also have a mark on our back door?" asked Rachel.

Mama laughed and kissed Rachel and stroked her hot forehead. "It does seem so, doesn't it?" she said.

"Cats and tramps and what else?" asked Rachel.

Mama laughed. "Call in Mr. Pye," she said, the way they all always did when they couldn't find any logical answer to a question.

13

The Yellow Hat Again

Jerry and Rachel continued to be on the lookout for the man with the yellow hat for they were sure that where they saw the hat they would likewise see Ginger.

This important day was the twenty-ninth of May, a sort of a holiday because it was Jerry's birthday. It happened also to be a Saturday. Early in the morning Rachel and Jerry set out to explore the great field below the railroad station for wild strawberries which usually grew there in abundance and which they were very fond of, crushed up with milk and sugar. They would surprise Uncle Bennie with a cupful of these when he arrived for his regular Saturday morning visit which was going to be an all-day visit since it was Jerry's birthday.

The field was still wet with dew and it was covered with juicy little ripe berries. Rachel and Jerry

filled three cups besides eating a great quantity as they picked. They tasted so good they then ate all they had picked except Uncle Bennie's. They were tired of picking any more and since Uncle Bennie was so very little and probably could not eat a whole cupful they then ate half of his. Now they had none left to eat with milk and sugar but this did not really matter since it was Jerry's birthday and they might be going to have ice cream.

A scraggy hill covered with pale wild roses led

up to the railroad station and they clambered up it, for they imagined they were just in time to see the Banker's Express go roaring by. Naturally the Banker's Express never stopped in Cranbury. But Jerry and Rachel loved to watch the speedy train whenever they could and wave to the engineer and the passengers, and catch a glimpse of people eating in the dining car, not just sandwiches they had packed—real bacon and eggs and coffee on beautiful white tablecloths. Why the coffee stayed on the tables instead of slopping all over the people and onto the aisles was a mystery, the fast way the train went. Anyway it must or so many people would not eat in this dangerous fashion.

The railroad station was one of their most favorite places in the entire town of Cranbury. While waiting for the Banker's Express they got weighed on the baggage scales several times. They shook the peanut machine and the gum machine for stray pennies, peanuts, and gum. Then they got weighed again, with and without their sweaters on. Then they went back out on the platform for, according to the clock, it was about time for the Banker's Express.

"Lookit the way the railroad tracks meet way off there," said Jerry.

"Um-m," said Rachel. "That's perspective," she said, for she had just learned this in school.

"Um-m-m," agreed Jerry. "Perspective."

Then, into the perspective, there came a little dot and it grew rapidly larger and larger with a line of smoke following along above it.

"Here it comes!" shouted Jerry.

"Here comes the Banker's Express!" shouted Rachel, and they both stood back expecting to see the train go streaking by the way it always did. But the train didn't streak by. It slowed up and did an unheard-of thing for the Banker's Express. It stopped. In Cranbury where it never stopped, it nonetheless stopped. It came to a standstill in such a way that the last coach was at the platform where Jerry and Rachel were standing. Being a very long train the front of it must be almost out to the reservoir, Rachel and Jerry imagined.

The train lurched backwards and forwards for a few moments as though in perplexity as to what to do. Then it stopped again.

"It's getting water or something," Jerry explained.

Jerry and Rachel were so excited watching the important train lurch forward and backward and do such an odd thing as stop here at the Cranbury railroad station that they did not notice a big boy standing on the rear platform. But this boy noticed them and he was watching them intently and maybe it was his dark glowering glance that finally made them look at him. Good night! It was Wally Bullwinkle! Wally Bullwinkle, with no hat on, on the Banker's Express!

"Where ya going, Wally?" yelled Jerry.

"Going to New York, Wally?" asked Rachel.

"Going to the Museum of Natural History?" asked Jerry.

Wally met these friendly questions with a surly grimace. He thrust out his lower lip and looked as though he would like to pick a fight.

"What are you mad at?" asked Jerry curiously.

Wally answered something, but what he said they never knew for at this moment the train slowly and evenly began to move. Wally slapped a hat on his head. And there he stood, Wally Bullwinkle, with an old yellow hat on, on the Banker's Express! But a gust of wind snatched Wally's hat off and though he tried to grab it, it was no use, the hat was gone.

Wally's hat landed on the platform and rolled to Jerry's feet. It was an old yellow felt hat on the order of the one the unsavory character had worn. Jerry looked at the hat and he looked at the train, gathering speed now, with Wally clinging to the back railing with one hand and feeling his bare head

with the other in bewilderment. Then the train disappeared around the bend and the Banker's Express, with Wally Bullwinkle on it, was gone.

Rachel and Jerry stared at the hat and they stared at each other, and Rachel said breathlessly, "He did have an old yellow hat after all. Wasn't spots before our eyes at the skeleton house. Was a hat like Unsavory's."

Jerry picked up the hat. Neither he nor Rachel yet connected *this* yellow hat that belonged to Wally Bullwinkle, a boy in Jerry's class and the owner of a dog as ferocious, so Wally claimed, as the one that bit the nose off Bit-nose Ned, with the yellow hat of Unsavory whose picture they had drawn so often as the villain in the story of the disappearance of Ginger Pye. Jerry said, "We'll save his old hat for him for when he comes back."

Rachel said, "It looked like Wally was going away for good. He had a going-away-for-good look about him."

"Oh-h-h," said Jerry slowly with remembering. "He might be. He said in the schoolyard the other day that he and his pop—he hasn't any mother—were going to join a vaudeville show. They'd been training for it, he said. It's what his pop used to do, he said. We didn't believe him, Dick Badger and me, because he's always saying something ain't true."

"He might have an act with that fierce dog he owns," said Rachel.

And then suddenly the same thought struck both of them. The fierce dog might be a ruse. The dog for the act might be Ginger!

"The hat!" screamed Rachel. "Has it got the mark in it? The mark, you know, the red mark?"

Muttering, "Of course not. This is Wally's old hat, not the unsavory character's," still Jerry paled and he took the hat into the bright sunshine and he turned down the inside band and there, sure enough! there was the red crayon mark just where Dick Badger had put it that day at the reservoir. And there Wally Bullwinkle was, on the Banker's Express, and perhaps he was leaving the town of Cranbury forever. And all along he probably was the one who had stolen Ginger and not the villain they had drawn the picture of. And was Ginger on the train too? In the baggage car? And did this mean they would never ever see their dog, Ginger, again?

"He might still not have been the one," murmured Rachel. "He might be one of a yellow-hat band of people and not be *the* one," she said. "Like I said."

"No," said Jerry. "No."

They both stared down the silent shimmering tracks where the train with Wally had gone. "We could catch the next train," suggested Rachel. "And trail him in New York."

She knew this was impossible, but she had to think of something. "Could we have him apprehended in New York?" she wondered.

There must be something they could do. *Call in Mr. Pye*, thought Rachel and she said they better hurry home and ask Papa what to do anyway. Papa might go to New York himself and bump into Wally on the escalator the way he had Mama. He would do something.

Jerry and Rachel started to race for home as fast as they could go, forgetting to whoop under the bridge they were so excited. They were sure their dog, Ginger, was on the Banker's Express and, though he was, they thought, at this very moment being whisked off to New York, still they felt nearer to him than at any time since his disappearance. Jerry held the old yellow hat firmly in his hands. It was a really close link with Ginger, he thought.

"You know what," said Jerry, panting. "First, before we go home, we better go over to Wally's house and see if by any chance Ginger was left behind, see if there is any trace of him or the big fierce dog or what."

So they changed their course. On the corner of Elm and New Dollar Street, whom should they see coming marching up the street with a hard firm step but Chief Larrimer on his way home for his coffee and buns. When he heard the latest developments in the Ginger Pye case, he turned around and joined Rachel and Jerry in the reconnoitering of the Bullwinkle homestead.

Jerry was very proud to be walking along the streets of Cranbury with the policeman but Rachel was wondering if people were thinking she and Jerry had been arrested. Then she decided, no, people would not think this since neither she nor Jerry had handcuffs on and she danced along sometimes a little ahead of the policeman sometimes a little behind to accent the fact of their freedom.

"The Bullwinkles, eh?" said Chief Larrimer, breaking the silence. "A shiftless lot, the father is. And like father, like son," he said.

When they reached Wally Bullwinkle's house it looked smaller and more shrunken than it ever used to because it was all boarded up. A "For Sale" sign was tacked in a lopsided fashion on the front. Despite the house's closed-up look Chief Larrimer tramped up on the porch and knocked at the door. Presently, the street in front of the house was filled with curious onlookers, chiefly children, though women and men gathered too.

Without turning around Chief Larrimer called

for a hammer and a small ax. In no time at all a half dozen or more of these were offered him. And Chief Larrimer pried off the boarding from one of the front windows and in he stepped, telling Jerry and Rachel they might come too and identify their dog, if he was here, which he didn't think was so, but who could be sure of anything? Not a policeman, they cannot jump to conclusions, he said, though it was all right to follow up a good hunch.

Everybody else, outside, wanted to come in, too, but permission was not granted. So they stayed without, waiting for a little something to be said to satisfy their curiosity.

Chief Larrimer, followed by Rachel and Jerry, went from room to room. Meager furniture stood in each room. There was certainly no dog in this house, no live one that is, for there were plenty of pictures of dogs and posters of dogs and most of these were of the circus and vaudeville variety, doing this trick and that, jumping through hoops and everything. Still, from the look of the place, the Bullwinkles had gone for good, or at least for a long, long time.

"The backyard, now," said Chief Larrimer. And he pushed open the flimsy back door. He was so strong, he needed no hammer or ax for this and the three inspectors found themselves in a high-fenced

small yard with a shed in one corner. There was barbed wire on top of the fence and there were a number of huge signs, on the shed, on the fences, on the house itself, saying, "Big Dog. Keep out!" and "Beware of the Big Dog!"

"Those are to throw you off the track," said Chief Larrimer. "Your dog being little."

In the little shed, which was open, they found any number of old gnawed bones, a little pile of rags with some ginger-colored hairs on them, and also, again, any number of vaudeville and circus posters, all with dogs on them, dogs on the order of Ginger, if Ginger were a big dog and not a little puppy. There was a broken strand of frayed rope tied to a hook. Here Ginger must have been kept. Here he must have slept and eaten and, perhaps, cried for Jerry and Rachel to come and find him.

Jerry picked up some of the old rags Ginger must have slept on. While feeling proud that, like detectives, he could identify the hairs of his dog, remembering the color so well, a terrible lump was gathering in his throat. For Ginger was gone, yet had been here all the while. It probably was Ginger he had heard whining that night he and Rachel came to the skeleton house. They had been right all along that Ginger was nearer to them over here where first they heard the mysterious footsteps.

"You threw me off, lad, with that picture you drewed of the man," said Chief Larrimer.

"We threwed ourselves and all of us off the track," admitted Jerry ruefully. "We didn't know an unsavory character could be just a boy in my class. We thought it had to be a man."

"Wally did have a yellow hat on that night we saw him at the skeleton house," said Rachel. "It wasn't spots before our eyes or hats in our belfry, it was Wally."

Chief Larrimer twirled his nightstick and looked important. "Skeleton houses," he said, pondering.

"Even if we had been sure it was a hat like the hat of the unsavory character, we would not have thought Wally was the unsavory character himself. We thought there might be a band of yellow-hat wearers and he, Wally, might be under the spell of a Fagin."

"Fagin?" said Chief Larrimer.

"Sir. Chief," said Jerry. "Rachel once thought some perfectly good tomatoes were poisoned tomatoes and we had to bury them."

"I see," said Chief Larrimer, but he looked confused. "I like to stick to facts," he said. "As I see it, the Bullwinkles with your dog have gone. They've gone to join a circus, I would deduce."

"Gone," murmured Jerry. "My dog . . ."

"We will have the train watched from New York to Boston," promised the able, new policeman. "And from Boston to New York," he added, for anyone could see that Jerry and Rachel felt very badly. "Let the Bullwinkles try to come back to Cranbury," he said. He said he would lock the father up for stealing a dog and perhaps maltreating him. He was a villain, an unsavory character, a black blot on Cranbury and he was not welcome here. They had not had to use the jail in ten years. But let the Bullwinkles come back and they would use the jail now, all right, and he, for one—and he was sure Judge Ball would concur—hoped they would use it for a good long time, ten years maybe.

Sadly, Rachel and Jerry followed the policeman back through the house and out the front door again to the waiting throng. They didn't care about jail and the ten years there. All they wanted was Ginger back again. That was all. And that was everything to them.

"Go home," bade the policeman to the curious bystanders. "Disband. A dog is gone."

The crowd disbanded. "A dog is gone," they said, satisfied with this tidbit but disappointed it was not a murder.

Jerry and Rachel said good-bye to the policeman

in front of Judge Ball's house where their ways parted. They were so choked up they could not even thank Chief Larrimer for skipping his coffee and buns to come reconnoitering.

" 'Bye," they said. They didn't even remember anymore that it was Jerry's birthday and that they might have ice cream. But, once they had parted from Chief Larrimer, they tore for home anyway. Thoughts of Ginger speeding away on the Banker's Express put speed in their toes too. Papa just had to think of what to do next. It was all right for Chief Larrimer to say he'd have all trains watched from New York to Boston and from Boston to New York. It was circuses that had to be watched now, they thought.

Chief Larrimer's ideas were all right as far as they went. He was a wonderful Chief of Police to have kept the jail empty the way Chief Mulligan, before him, had done, too, for ten years. This showed how orderly they had both kept the town of Cranbury so far. But ideas of a more dramatic nature were necessary now, the kind of ideas Papa must have every second or the men in Washington would not be forever saying, "Call in Mr. Pye."

That was the sort of thinking Rachel and Jerry were doing as they rounded the corner, skidding the way Ginger used to, they were going so fast, and sprinted, panting, down Beam's Place to home.

During these exciting adventures they had lost all of Uncle Bennie's berries but not the cups.

14

Uncle Bennie, Hero

When Jerry and Rachel drew near their house on Beam's Place they stopped short in amazement for a very extraordinary sight greeted them. There were Mama and Papa and Gramma and Uncle Bennie all standing around on the Pyes' front lawn under the chestnut tree. And there was a strange dog tearing around and around in wider and wider circles, snorting painfully, acting half mad.

In wonder, feeling like outsiders to this family picture in which they had no part—for, obviously, a great moment in the Pye family was taking place, as great a moment, perhaps, as that of Papa running up the "down" escalator—Jerry and Rachel slowly drew nearer. Then the strange dog spied them and he raced to them. He leaped in the air in front of them, half crying, half barking with joy, licking their faces, whimpering, talking the best he knew how.

He was a full-grown dog, a fox terrier, and he was brown-and-white.

For a moment Jerry and Rachel were speechless as the truth dawned on them. In their minds it had been so firmly fixed that Ginger Pye was on the Banker's Express, it did not seem possible that this might be he, here on Beam's Place. Still, all of a sudden, the truth, like skyrockets, burst upon them and first Jerry and then Rachel cried, "Ginger! Ginger!"

For it was Ginger! They could tell it was by the odd crooked marking on his back. They knew it was Ginger. Ginger was back and they hugged him and petted him and kissed him. It was big Ginger, not little Ginger pup anymore.

It was funny but all the long months that Ginger had been gone, everyone still thought of him as a little puppy such as he had been when he had disappeared. Of course he would have been growing and growing all this time but everyone had forgotten that he would be doing this. But so he had. And this was Ginger, and he was not on the Banker's Express going heavens knew where, to what circus and what strange lands. He was right here in the Pyes' own front yard and he was beside himself with joy and so were they.

"I found him! I found him!" yelled Uncle Bennie. "I tojer I'd find him. I found Ginger. I was looking for Friskies and the Japanese and I found Ginger. He ran up to me and kissed me. I found him."

Ginger had a long, frayed, shaggy, broken-off rope tied to his collar that was exactly like the piece of rope in Wally Bullwinkle's shed. "Where'd he come from? Where'd he come from?" asked Jerry and Rachel excitedly. They wanted to tell all about the Banker's Express and the policeman but first they wanted to know how Ginger got to be here when they thought he was on the way to New York. So Gramma, with corrections and interruptions from Uncle Bennie, explained what had happened as far as she knew Uncle Bennie's and her end of the story. They had already explained it to Mama and Papa but, of course, they were happy to explain it all over again to Rachel and Jerry.

Well. As Gramma and Uncle Bennie were on their way over here—they had left very early, just a little after seven because Uncle Bennie was impatient to get to Jerry and the birthday house and he hoped the ice cream was going to be steamboats again—and as they were walking along Second Avenue near the big new house, Uncle Bennie said,

"Down, down." That meant he wanted to get out of his express wagon and chase the Friskies and the Japanese, his words for butterflies.

So Gramma stopped and Uncle Bennie climbed out and he went chasing butterflies from hedge to hedge and bush to bush while she drew his empty squeaking wagon behind her.

Suddenly they heard a frantic barking and yelping, like a dog in terrible pain. They thought perhaps a dog had been run over and while they were looking around to see, why, the next thing they knew, this strange dog came bounding out from some yard behind them. Gramma could not tell which house, but she knew the general direction.

"Wally Bullwinkle's," murmured Rachel in awe at the way things, like the frayed rope on Ginger's neck, were being pieced together.

"Sh-sh," said Jerry. "There's more."

Gramma went on with the explaining.

"It's Ginger. It's Ginger!" Uncle Bennie had yelled and the dog kept jumping up on Uncle Bennie and kissing him. But Gramma thought this was just a dog, just any dog. She didn't realize it was Ginger because she still thought of Ginger the way they all did, as being a tiny little puppy. So she said, "Go back, doggy. Nice doggy, go back."

But the dog didn't want to go back. Whenever

Gramma said, "Go back," to him, he cringed and
slunk on the ground. The minute they went on a
few paces he bounded along eagerly and happily
with them. Gramma thought, "My, what a friendly
dog!" He kept jumping up on her, trying to kiss her,
and he kept licking her hands and he behaved the
same way with Uncle Bennie. It was as though he
was trying to tell them something, the way he whimpered and barked.

"It's Ginger! It's Ginger!" Uncle Bennie kept
yelling over and over.

But Gramma still did not think this was possible,
first, because she remembered Ginger as such a
little puppy, and second, because she really thought,

though she had never told them so, that Jerry and Rachel would never see their little dog again. She, long ago, thought he must be dead.

So she said hesitantly to Uncle Bennie, "No. This is not Ginger. This dog is too big." And again she said, "Go home, doggy."

But the dog would not go back. He would stop for a moment, pretending to obey her, and then he would prance up behind them, following them, and dragging his long broken rope behind him.

"This, Ginger," Uncle Bennie insisted positively. "I told Jerry and 'Achel I'd find Ginger. And I did," he said with satisfaction.

The dog kept knocking Uncle Bennie over, he was so happy and appreciative of being recognized, but Uncle Bennie was too delighted to mind the bumps. "Ginger, Ginger," he murmured over and over.

So Gramma finally said, "Well, let him come along with us and see what the folks think. If it is not Ginger, we'll bring him back here tonight."

"This poor Ginger. This ow-ow Ginger," said Uncle Bennie sadly.

Gramma had already noticed the terrible wound on the dog's forehead and she really didn't want him to go back anyway to people who mistreated him.

So she picked up the rope, and she and the dog and Uncle Bennie started as fast as they could go down Second Avenue, on their way again to the Pyes'.

"But then," said Gramma—she was as excited as the rest—"an odd thing happened. The Second Avenue trolley came along behind us, the one going to town, and it stopped right beside us, right in the middle of the block and a man and a boy leaned out the back door and yelled at us. They said, 'Hey. That's our dog. Bring him here.' But the dog broke loose from me and ran in someone's backyard— hiding, he was. The two of them on the trolley argued with the motorman then. They wanted him to stay there while they caught their dog, or sent him home or something. But the motorman said, 'They's more than you that wants to catch the Banker's Express. Stay on or get off.' And he just started up, he did, and off the trolley went, the man and the boy leaning out the back window all the way up the street and looking very disturbed and angry. The minute the car was out of sight—it stopped for Judge Ball and that was all—the dog came running back to us, trembling and quivering. I put two and two together," said Gramma, "and figured those people owned him and treated him meanly, the way he acted."

"That was Wally Bullwinkle and his father," interrupted Jerry excitedly.

"On their way to the Banker's Express," added Rachel, almost overcome at the way the story was working out.

"So, here we are," said Gramma.

They had arrived here right after Rachel and Jerry had left for the strawberry hunt. And of course the minute they got in sight of the Pyes' house the dog was nearly frantic with joy. And of course Mama and Papa recognized him immediately by the odd marking on his back and they said, "Uncle Bennie is right. This *is* Ginger!"

"What under the sun kept you so long?" they asked Rachel and Jerry. "We thought you'd never get here."

So now everyone had to hear Rachel and Jerry's side of the story, all about the Banker's Express, and its stopping, and Wally Bullwinkle on it, and the yellow hat, which same hat Jerry was still holding in his hands, and about the Chief of Police and the reconnoitering of Wally Bullwinkle's house, and the circus posters and the crowd outside, and Ginger's tawny hair on the old rags, and the frayed end of rope that matched the rope he had on now, the barbed wire, everything!

Gramma said, "Imagine! Imagine! He heard Uncle Bennie's squeaky cart and he recognized it!"

They all marveled at the smart dog that Ginger was, to have recognized Uncle Bennie's squeaky cart, just the sound of it.

"He probably heard us every Saturday and longed for a chance to make his escape," said Gramma. And she said, now that she thought of it, she had frequently heard a dog whining over there in that

part of Second Avenue, but she had never given it a minute's thought. Gramma was not as familiar with all the sounds that Ginger made as Jerry and Rachel were, or she would have known it was Ginger. If she had only commented! But she just naturally thought it was only one of the many dogs who lived over there. Practically every house had some dog or other living in it, and since she never saw this dog that whimpered, how would she possible have known that it was Ginger all the time?

None of them could get over it! To think that Ginger had, no doubt, heard Uncle Bennie's squeaky cart every Saturday and had never been able to get to Gramma and Uncle Bennie! To think of him straining and tearing at his rope, every Saturday morning probably, trying to get away, whining and whimpering to make Gramma hear. And Gramma hearing but not realizing that there, behind the barbed wire and the sheds and the posters and the Bullwinkle house, was Ginger! It was enough to make anybody cry, and they all gulped down the lumps in their throats. Somehow though, on this day when the Bullwinkles had planned to take him away once and for all, he had made the supreme effort and eluded them.

Perhaps that was how he had hurt his head,

jumping over the barbed wire. Awful as it was to think of Ginger hurting his head on the barbed wire, they hoped that was the way it happened and not that he had been mistreated. But that he had been mistreated also they did not doubt. Otherwise he would have grown fond of his new master after all this time and he would have forgotten the Pyes since he had been such a little puppy when he was stolen.

Moreover, they all noticed the yellow hat. Jerry had been secretly hurt and worried because it seemed to him that Ginger was not as happy to see him as he was the others. He had jumped up and kissed him once or twice, but he acted rather scared, though with the others he was delirious with joy. At first Jerry thought, *He is sore at me for not finding him when he found me in school, with my pencil.* Then, suddenly, Jerry remembered he was holding Wally Bullwinkle's yellow hat and he dropped it on the ground. Immediately Ginger leaped in his arms and stayed there at least two minutes, kissing him and crying. When he began running around again they all noticed how every time Ginger came anywhere near the yellow hat, he plastered his little bit of tail down and whimpered and skulked on the ground.

This was final proof, if any more proof were needed, that it was Wally who had kidnapped Ginger, since Wally was the owner of this yellow hat and likewise the person Gramma had seen on the Second Avenue trolley claiming Ginger was his. And now they all speculated on what might have happened if today had not happened to be Jerry's birthday and Uncle Bennie and Gramma had not left home earlier than usual to come to the Pyes'. Then Ginger would certainly at this moment be on the Banker's Express, tearing to New York and perhaps the far West with Wally Bullwinkle, gone for good.

What a joyous reunion this was! Joyous and sad all at once. It was joyous, of course, because Ginger was back. But it was sad because Ginger had the dreadful raw sore on his forehead indicating he had either been mistreated or else had been badly torn making his escape over the barbed wire. The gash was so deep Mama was afraid the fur would never grow back over it again. So Ginger, and all of them, would have always the reminder of his terrible kidnapping and stay with the mean Bullwinkles.

Jerry and Rachel cried. They had not cried in public when Ginger was stolen. But they cried now, seeing his hurting head. They couldn't love Ginger enough to make up for all the long months he had gone without loving. And they just couldn't get over the whole thing, how here he was a full-grown dog now that had been such a little puppy when he was stolen on Thanksgiving Day. And yet he remembered and loved them all still. He was a wonderful, wonderful dog.

Ginger licked their tears away and Gracie-the-cat, when Ginger, panting, finally lay down to rest a moment, licked his wounded face. But Ginger did not rest long. He had to tear around and tear around again to show how happy he was. And he was still just as smart as ever.

"Look at that, will you?" said tall Sam Doody, coming up with his camera at this moment and joining in with the exclaiming and the marveling and the piecing together of the story. "Look at that dog, will you?" For Ginger was doing another thing as smart as finding Jerry in school and recognizing Uncle Bennie's squeaky cart.

The tar wagon had been over the street while Rachel and Jerry had been strawberry hunting and Beam's Place was sticky and shining with tar. The smell of tar was everywhere. Gracie-the-cat had occasion to wish to get to the other side of the street. This was obvious to all of them because she kept going to the gutter, sticking a paw tentatively in the edge of the tar and meowing unhappily and disapprovingly. She wanted to get across the street but she was too fastidious about stepping in tar to do so.

Ginger watched her quizzically, his head on one

side, taking in the balking situation. Then he gave
an impatient snort and grabbed Gracie by the nape
of the neck and ran across the tarry road with her.
He didn't mind his toes getting black, but she minded
hers getting black. This way, she stayed neat and
tidy. Then, when Gracie wanted to come back—
which she did immediately, meowing forlornly at
them all the minute Ginger deposited her on the
other side—Ginger ran across and grabbed her up
again by the nape of the neck and brought her back.
Gracie-the-cat was astonished and so were all of
them.

He was the smartest dog any of them had ever
seen or read about anywhere to do such a thing as

that. He had been a smart puppy and now he was a smart dog. Sam Doody snapped a couple of pictures of Ginger crossing the tar with Gracie, but since the dog and the cat were moving so fast he didn't expect the pictures would amount to much.

Ginger just picked up life right where it had left off for him back on Thanksgiving Day. It almost seemed as though there should be the smell of roast chicken in the air, and drumsticks to pick on. Ginger scratched Gracie's fleas, dashed for the orange duster, and brought Jerry rocks to throw for him. It turned out that while Ginger had been gone he had learned a great number of new tricks which Jerry and Rachel and Uncle Bennie learned about gradually. For instance, he could stand on his front paws and he could also turn a somersault.

"You don't have to do any tricks," said Jerry, hugging him. "Just so you're back. That's all I care. You don't ever have to do one more trick." He could not bear to think that perhaps the terrible scar on Ginger's forehead was caused by a blow given him when he was being taught a new trick Wally and his father expected to use in vaudeville or the circus.

Ginger's eyes had always been beautiful, gay, sparkling, laughing, and intelligent. Now they were even more beautiful for there were sadness and pleading, an anxious questioning, in them, too. It was all any of them could do not to cry when they looked into Ginger's eyes and each one vied with the others saying endearing words to him, and petting him, to make up for all the sadness he had suffered shut up in that miserable Bullwinkle shed while, all along, they had been comfortable in their nice warm house.

To think he had never been allowed out of Wally's little yard, even, for a good brisk run. Naturally, since he was a stolen dog, Wally had had to keep him under lock and key.

"Oh, Ginger, oh, Ginger," sobbed Rachel, every now and then, kissing his wounded hurting head.

"All the times we were right down there, calling him and looking for him!" said Jerry.

"Big dog! Keep out!" said Rachel indignantly. "Wally was probably holding his fist over Ginger's mouth every time he saw us coming."

"Ginger probably heard us and knew we were right there," said Jerry.

"Well," comforted Mrs. Pye. "That helped him to remember you and keep you in mind until the right moment came for his escape."

Anyway, sad as Ginger's life had been while he was away, he was—from now on—the happiest dog in Cranbury, and Jerry and Rachel and Uncle Bennie were the happiest children, since he was back. They did love him so.

It got to be noontime. The children all had some dinner and then they had ice cream. Ginger had some too. But the children didn't even realize they were eating ice cream, they were so excited. If there had been lumps of frozen peach in it as at Gramma's, they might have known. But there weren't lumps. This was bought ice cream though not steamboats, pickaxes, or robins.

Sam Doody had some ice cream too, and so did the Chief of Police. He came by just then, having had his buns and coffee at last, to make a report on latest developments. When the Pyes could finally persuade Ginger to stop barking at him, Chief Larrimer said, "I telephoned down the line when I got home. And I ordered the Banker's Express stopped and searched in Westport. Your dog is not on it," he said.

Chief Larrimer was not yet aware that the dog who had been barking at him was the long-missing, famous Ginger. When he was told this, and that the quest was ended, he looked a shade disappointed. It was obvious that he had other plans, such as ordering all dogs in shows examined carefully to see if they might be Ginger. However, Jerry and Rachel looked at him so admiringly—he had, after all, thought of marvelous ways of tracing their dog, having the Banker's Express itself stopped, for example—that the Chief's ruffled spirits were smoothed.

Nevertheless, in case the Chief might feel it was a reflection on his office that Ginger had not been found by him, but had been found by Uncle Bennie, a three-year-old, one of Cranbury's youngest citizens, he said, "The young-uns threw me off the track with that picture they drewed of the man."

"We thought Wally Bullwinkle was just a boy in my class," explained Jerry apologetically, for now it seemed as though, from the beginning, it should have been as plain as the nose on his face that Wally *had* been the thief. "We didn't know Wally was a thief and he didn't look like the picture we drew of the unsavory character. We didn't know an unsavory character could be just a boy in my class," said Jerry.

"Wally hasn't any mother," said Rachel. She didn't want Wally to go to jail. She wanted someone to be nice to him and make him nice. "His father probably didn't know he had stolen Ginger," she said, making excuses for Mr. Bullwinkle also.

"That may well be," said Chief Larrimer. "But if you have any more thefts," he said, "don't draw me the thief." And he tramped off up the street, having to get to the bank before it closed.

The next who came by were Mr. Badger and Dick Badger and Duke. They had been out in Cheshire and missed all the excitement. Mr. Badger wanted some pictures for the *Cranbury Chronicle* and Sam Doody took them. One picture he took he called "A happy reunion." It showed all the family gathered around Ginger while Ginger scratched the fleas of Gracie-the-cat. Another picture he took of just Uncle Bennie and Ginger. Sam Doody named Uncle Bennie "The hero of the day." Uncle Bennie had

been a hero before, just for being an uncle at the
age of three. Now he was a hero also for being the
one to find Ginger.

For it was Uncle Bennie, after all, who insisted
that Ginger was Ginger and had persuaded Gramma
to let him follow them to the Pyes'. "I knews it was
Ginger," he affirmed importantly.

The picture that Sam Doody took of Uncle Bennie and Ginger would win the fifteen-dollar prize. That was what Jerry and Rachel thought. Not the pictures of East Rock at all, not even the G N U one which turned out to be a beauty.

"Uncle Bennie, Uncle Bennie, Uncle Bennie!" they all exclaimed affectionately. "Uncle Bennie, hero."

Uncle Bennie beamed.

How the day passed no one knew. But at last the great birthday day, the sort of a holiday, the day of Ginger Pye's dramatic return, came to an end. Everyone had gone, all the guests, the interested neighbors, Uncle Bennie, and Gramma. And it was night, that first night that Ginger was home and curled up sleeping on Jerry's feet as he used to; and there was, in the distance, the wonderful occasional sound of the trains running from New York to Boston, from Boston to New York; and Jerry said it first. He said, comfortably, hoping she was not asleep, "Rachel . . ."

"Um-m-m," said Rachel, squirming delightedly. She knew what was coming.

"Oh, Boombernickles," said Jerry. "Oh, Martin Boombernickles."

Rachel laughed softly. "Yes," she said. "And

then what happened?" Just as though they had never stopped.

Ginger twitched his ears and the loose skin on his back and legs to let Jerry know he was here and he was happy. Then he lowered his head down on his paws again and he let out a deep sigh that sounded almost like a sob, there was in it so much relief and pain and pleasure and remembering.

Eleanor Estes (1906–1988) grew up in West Haven, Connecticut, which she renamed Cranbury for her classic stories about the Moffat and Pye families. A children's librarian for many years, she launched her writing career with the publication of *The Moffats* in 1941. Two of her outstanding books about the Moffats—*Rufus M.* and *The Middle Moffat*—were awarded Newbery Honors, as was her short novel *The Hundred Dresses*. She won the Newbery Medal for *Ginger Pye* in 1952. The inspiration for Ginger Pye, the "intellectual dog," came from a real dog who appeared, pencil in mouth, in the window of the ivy-covered school of Eleanor Estes's childhood.